**"POWERFUL AND ELECTRIFYING."**
—Colin Wilson

The snipers zero in on us. Each shot becomes a word spoken by death. Death is talking to us. Death wants to tell us a funny secret. We may not like death but death likes us. Victor Charlie is hard but he never lies. Guns tell the truth. Guns never say, "I'm only kidding." War is ugly because the truth can be ugly and war is very sincere.

### THE SHORT-TIMERS

**"BRILLIANT."**

—*Chicago Tribune Book World*

**"ARRESTING."**

—*Atlantic Monthly*

**"EXTRAORDINARY."**

—*Philadelphia Inquirer*

Praise for
*THE SHORT-TIMERS*

*The Short-Timers*, a leatherneck version of *Catch-22*,[1] is a first novel and it is extraordinary.[2] Hasford knows his subject.[3] The driving and often brilliant first-person narrative[4] carries you out of your chair and deposits you into the clatter of a jungle patrol.[5] The writing is crisp and tough. There is an enormous feeling of horror.[6] Arresting,[7] disturbing,[8] often very funny,[9] honest and accurate,[10] chock full of undeniable truths, *The Short-Timers* is a savage, unforgiving look at a savage, unforgivable time.[11]

Read it if you dare.[12]

**"POWERFUL AND ELECTRIFYING."**
—Colin Wilson

[1]*San Gabriel Highlander.* [2]*Philadelphia Inquirer.* [3]*Washington Post.* [4]*Chicago Tribune Book World.* [5]*San Diego Union.* [6]*Star-Ledger* (Newark). [7]*Atlantic Monthly.* [8]*Longview Daily News.* [9]*Figaro.* [10]*Sacramento Bee.* [11]*Los Angeles Times.* [12]*Jersey Journal.*

# THE
# SHORT-TIMERS

## GUSTAV HASFORD

**BANTAM BOOKS**
TORONTO • NEW YORK • LONDON • SYDNEY • AUCKLAND

THE SHORT-TIMERS
*A Bantam Book*

*PRINTING HISTORY*
*Harper & Row edition published January 1979*
*Bantam edition / February 1980*
*2nd printing .... January 1980*
*3rd printing ..... March 1980*
*4th printing ... December 1983*

ISBN 0-553-23945-7

*Published simultaneously in the United States and Canada*

*Bantam Books are published by Bantam Books, Inc. Its trade-
mark, consisting of the words "Bantam Books" and the por-
trayal of a rooster, is Registered in U.S. Patent and Trademark
Office and in other countries. Marca Registrada. Bantam
Books, Inc., 666 Fifth Avenue, New York, New York 10103.*

PRINTED IN THE UNITED STATES OF AMERICA

H     13 12 11 10 9

Dedicated to
        "Penny"
JOHN C. PENNINGTON, Corporal
Combat Photographer, First Marine Division
   KIA, June 9, 1968


## Adieu to a Soldier

Adieu, O soldier,
You of the rude campaigning, (which we shared,)
The rapid march, the life of the camp,
The hot contention of opposing fronts, the long manoêuvre,
Red battles with their slaughter, the stimulus, the strong
        terrific game,
Spell of all brave and manly hearts, the trains of time
        through you and like of you all fill'd,
With war and war's expression.

Adieu, dear comrade,
Your mission is fulfill'd—but I, more warlike,
Myself and this contentious soul of mine,
Still on our campaigning bound,
Through untried roads with ambushes opponents lined,
Through many a sharp defeat and many a crisis, often
        baffled,
Here marching, ever marching on, a war fight out—aye here,
To fiercer, weightier battles give expression.

                    WALT WHITMAN, *Drum Taps*, 1871

# THE SPIRIT OF
# THE BAYONET

*I think that Vietnam was what we had instead of happy childhoods.*

MICHAEL HERR, *Dispatches*

The Marines are looking for a few good men. . . .

The recruit says that his name is Leonard Pratt.

Gunnery Sergeant Gerheim takes one look at the skinny red-neck and immediately dubs him "Gomer Pyle."

We think maybe he's trying to be funny. Nobody laughs.

Dawn. Green Marines. Three junior drill instructors screaming, "GET IN LINE! GET IN LINE! YOU WILL NOT MOVE! YOU WILL NOT SPEAK!" Red brick buildings. Willow trees hung thick with Spanish moss. Long, irregular lines of sweating civilians standing tall on yellow footprints painted in a pattern on the concrete deck.

Parris Island, South Carolina, the United States Marine Corps Recruit Depot, an eight-week college for the phony-tough and the crazy-brave, constructed in a swamp on an island, symmetrical but sinister like a suburban death camp.

3

Gunnery Sergeant Gerheim spits. "Listen up, herd. You maggots had better start looking like United States Marine Corps recruits. Do not think for one second that you are Marines. You just dropped by to pick up a set of dress blues. Am I right, ladies? Sorry 'bout that."

A wiry little Texan in horn-rimmed glasses the guys are already calling "Cowboy" says, "Is that you, John Wayne? Is this me?" Cowboy takes off his pearl-gray Stetson and fans his sweaty face.

I laugh. Years of high school drama classes have made me a mimic. I sound exactly like John Wayne as I say: "I think I'm going to hate this movie."

Cowboy laughs. He beats his Stetson on his thigh.

Gunnery Sergeant Gerheim laughs, too. The senior drill instructor is an obscene little ogre in immaculate khaki. He aims his index finger between my eyes and says, "*You.* Yeah—*you.* Private Joker. I like you. You can come over to my house and fuck my sister." He grins. Then his face goes hard. "You little scumbag. I got your name. I got your ass. You *will not* laugh. You *will not* cry. You will learn by the numbers. I will teach you."

Leonard Pratt grins.

Sergeant Gerheim puts his fists on his hips. "*If you ladies leave my island, if* you survive recruit training, you will be a weapon, you will be a minister of death, praying for war. And proud. Until that day you are pukes, you are scumbags, you are the lowest form of life on Earth. You are not even human. You people are nothing but a lot of little pieces of amphibian shit."

Leonard chuckles.

"Private Pyle thinks I am a real funny guy. He

4

thinks that Parris Island is more fun than a sucking chest wound."

The hillbilly's face is frozen into a permanent expression of oat-fed innocence.

"You maggots are not going to have any fun here. You are not going to enjoy standing in straight lines and you are not going to enjoy massaging your own wand and you are not going to enjoy saying 'sir' to individuals you do not like. Well, ladies, that's tough titty. I will speak and you will function. Ten percent of you will not survive. Ten percent of you maggots are going to go AWOL or will try to take your own lives or will break your backs on the Confidence Course or will just go plain fucking crazy. There it is. My orders are to weed out all nonhackers who do not pack the gear to serve in my beloved Corps. You will be grunts. Grunts get no slack. My recruits learn to survive without slack. Because I am hard, you will not like me. But the more you hate me, the more you will learn. Am I correct, herd?"

Some of us mumble, "Yes. Yeah. Yes, sir."

"I can't *hear* you, ladies."

"Yes, sir."

"I *still* can't hear you, ladies. SOUND OFF LIKE YOU GOT A PAIR"

"YES, SIR!"

"You piss me off. Hit the deck."

We crumple down onto the hot parade deck.

"You got no motivation. Do you hear me, maggots? Listen up. I will *give* you motivation. You have no esprit de corps. I will *give* you esprit de corps. You have no traditions. I will *give* you traditions. And I will show you how to live up to them."

Sergeant Gerheim struts, ramrod straight, hands on hips. "GET UP! GET UP!"

We get up, sweating, knees sore, hands gritty.

Sergeant Gerheim says to his three junior drill instructors: "What a humble herd." Then to us: "You silly scumbags are too *slow*. Hit the deck."

*Down.*

*Up.*

*Down.*

*Up.*

"HIT IT!"

*Down.*

Sergeant Gerheim steps over our struggling bodies, stomps fingers, kicks ribs with the toe of his boot. "Jesus H. Christ. You maggots are huffing and puffing the way your momma did the first time your old man put the meat to her."

*Pain.*

"GET UP! GET UP!"

*Up.* Muscles aching.

Leonard Pratt is still sprawled on the hot concrete. Sergeant Gerheim dances over to him, stands over him, shoves his Smokey the Bear campaign cover to the back of his bald head. "Okay, scumbag, *do* it."

Leonard gets up on one knee, hesitates, then stands up, inhaling and exhaling. He grins.

Sergeant Gerheim punches Leonard in the Adam's apple—*hard*. The sergeant's big fist pounds Leonard's chest. Then his stomach. Leonard doubles over with pain. "LOCK THEM HEELS! YOU'RE AT ATTENTION!" Sergeant Gerheim backhands Leonard across the face.

Blood.

Leonard grins, locks his heels. Leonard's lips are

busted, pink and purple, and his mouth is bloody, but Leonard only shrugs and grins as though Gunnery Sergeant Gerheim has just given him a birthday present.

For the first four weeks of recruit training Leonard continues to grin, even though he receives more than his share of the beatings. Beatings, we learn, are a routine element of life on Parris Island. And not that I'm-only-rough-on-'um-because-I-love-'um crap civilians have seen in Jack Webb's Hollywood movie *The D.I.* and in Mr. John Wayne's *The Sands of Iwo Jima.* Gunnery Sergeant Gerheim and his three junior drill instructors administer brutal beatings to faces, chests, stomachs, and backs. With fists. Or boots—they kick us in the ass, the kidneys, the ribs, any part of our bodies upon which a black and purple bruise won't show.

But even having the shit beat out of him with calculated regularity fails to educate Leonard the way it educates the other recruits in Platoon 30-92. In high-school psychology they said that fish, cockroaches, and even one-celled protozoa can be brainwashed. But not Leonard.

Leonard tries harder than any of us.

He can't do anything right.

During the day Leonard stumbles and falls, but never complains.

At night, as the platoon sleeps in double-tiered metal bunks, Leonard cries. I whisper to him to be quiet. He stops crying.

No recruit is ever allowed to be alone.

On the first day of our fifth week, Sergeant Gerheim beats the hell out of me.

7

I'm standing tall in Gerheim's palace, a small room at the far end of the squad bay.

"Do you believe in the Virgin Mary?"

"NO, SIR!" I say. It's a trick question. Any answer will be wrong, and Sergeant Gerheim will beat me harder if I reverse myself.

Sergeant Gerheim punches me in the solar plexus with his elbow. "You little maggot," he says, and his fist punctuates the sentence. I stand to attention, heels locked, eyes front, swallowing groans, trying not to flinch. "You make me want to vomit, scumbag. You goddamn heathen. You better sound off that you love the Virgin Mary or I'm going to stomp your guts out." Sergeant Gerheim's face is about one inch from my left ear. "EYES FRONT!" Spit sprinkles my cheek. "You *do* love the Virgin Mary, don't you, Private Joker? *Speak!*"

"SIR, NEGATIVE, SIR!"

I wait. I know that he is going to order me into the head. The shower stall is where he takes the recruits he wants to hurt. Almost every day recruits march into the head with Sergeant Gerheim and, because the deck in the shower stall is wet, they accidentally fall down. They accidentally fall down so many times that when they come out they look like they've been run over by a cat tractor.

He's behind me. I can hear him breathing.

"What did you say, prive?"

"SIR, THE PRIVATE SAID, 'NO, SIR!' SIR!"

Sergeant Gerheim's beefy red face floats by like a cobra being charmed by music. His eyes drill into mine; they invite me to look at him; they dare me to move my eyes one fraction of an inch.

"Have you seen the light? The white light? The great light? The guiding light—do you have the vision?"

"SIR, AYE-AYE, SIR!"

"Who's your squad leader, scumbag?"

"SIR, THE PRIVATE'S SQUAD LEADER IS PRIVATE HAMER, SIR!"

"Hamer, front and center."

Hamer runs down the center of the squad bay, snaps to attention in front of Sergeant Gerheim. "AYE-AYE, SIR!"

"Hamer, you're fired. Private Joker is promoted to squad leader."

Hamer hesitates. "AYE-AYE, SIR!"

"Go."

Hamer does an about-face, runs back down the squad bay, falls back into line in front of his rack, snaps to attention.

I say, "SIR, THE PRIVATE REQUESTS PERMISSION TO SPEAK TO THE DRILL INSTRUCTOR!"

"Speak."

"SIR, THE PRIVATE DOES NOT WANT TO BE A SQUAD LEADER, SIR!"

Gunnery Sergeant Gerheim puts his fists on his hips. He pushes his Smokey the Bear campaign cover to the back of his bald head. He sighs. "Nobody *wants* to lead, maggot, but somebody *has* to. You got the brain, you got the balls, so you get the job. The Marine Corps is not a mob like the Army. Marines die—that's what we're here for—but the Marine Corps will live forever, because every Marine is a leader when he has to be—even a prive."

Sergeant Gerheim turns to Leonard. "Private Pyle, Private Joker is your new bunkmate. Private Joker is a very bright boy. He will teach you everything. He will teach you how to pee."

I say, "SIR, THE PRIVATE WOULD PREFER TO STAY WITH HIS BUNKMATE, PRIVATE COWBOY, SIR!"

Cowboy and I have became friends because when you're far from home and scared shitless you need all the friends you can get and you need them right away. Cowboy is the only recruit who laughs at all my jokes. He's got a sense of humor, which is priceless in a place like this, but he's serious when he has to be —he's dependable.

Sergeant Gerheim sighs. "You queer for Private Cowboy's gear? You smoke his pole?"

"SIR, NEGATIVE, SIR!"

"Outstanding. Then Private Joker *will* bunk with Private Pyle. Private Joker is silly and he's ignorant, but he's got guts, and guts is enough."

Sergeant Gerheim struts back to his "palace," a tiny room at the far end of the squad bay. "Okay, ladies, ready . . . MOUNT !"

We all jump into our racks and freeze.

"Sing."

We sing:

> *From the halls of Montezuma,*
> *To the shores of Tripoli,*
> *We will fight our country's battles,*
> *On land, and air, and sea.*
>
> *If the Army and the Navy*
> *Ever gaze on heaven's scenes,*

*They will find the streets are guarded by
United States Marines . . .*

"Okay, herd, readdddy . . . SLEEP!"

Training continues.

I teach Leonard everything I know, from how to lace his black combat boots to the assembly and disassembly of the M-14 semi-automatic shoulder weapon.

I teach Leonard that Marines do not ditty-bop, they do not just walk. Marines run; they double-time. Or, if the distance to be covered is great, Marines hump, one foot after the other, one step at a time, for as long as necessary. Marines work hard. Only shitbirds try to avoid work, only shitbirds try to skate. Marines are clean, not skuzzy. I teach Leonard to value his rifle as he values his life. I teach him that blood makes the grass grow.

"This here gun is one mean-looking piece of iron, sure enough." Leonard's clumsy fingers snap his weapon together.

I'm repulsed by the look and feel of my own weapon. The rifle is cold and heavy in my hands. "Think of your rifle as a tool, Leonard. Like an ax on the farm."

Leonard grins. "Okay. You right, Joker." He looks at me. "I'm sure glad you're helping me, Joker. You're my friend. I know I'm slow. I always been slow. Nobody ever helped me. . . ."

I turn away. "That sounds like a personal problem," I say. I keep my eyes on my weapon.

Sergeant Gerheim continues the siege of Leonard Pratt, Private. He gives Leonard extra push-ups every night, yells at him louder than he yells at the rest of us, calls his mother more colorful names.

Meanwhile, the rest of us are not forgotten. We suffer, too. We suffer for Leonard's mistakes. We march, we run, we duck walk, and we crawl.

We play war in the swamp. Near the site of the Ribbon Creek Massacre, where six recruits drowned during a disciplinary night march in 1956, Sergeant Gerheim orders me to climb a willow tree. I'm a sniper. I'm supposed to shoot the platoon. I hang on a limb. If I can see a recruit well enough to name him, he's dead.

The platoon attacks. I yell, "HAMER!" and Hamer falls dead.

The platoon scatters. I scan the underbrush.

A green phantom blinks through a shadow. I see its face. I open my mouth. The limb cracks. I'm falling . . .

I collide with the sandy deck. I look up.

Cowboy is standing over me. "Bang, bang, you're dead," he says. And then he laughs.

Sergeant Gerheim looms over me. I try to explain that the limb broke.

"You can't talk, sniper. You are dead. Private Cowboy just took your life."

Sergeant Gerheim promotes Cowboy to squad leader.

During our sixth week, Sergeant Gerheim orders us to double-time around the squad bay with our penises in our left hands and our weapons in our right hands, singing: *This is my rifle, this is my gun; one is for fighting and one is for fun.* And: *I don't want no teen-aged queen; all I want is my M-14.*

Sergeant Gerheim orders us to name our rifles. "This is the only pussy you people are going to get. Your days of finger-banging ol' Mary Jane Rotten-crotch through her pretty pink panties are over. You're married to *this* piece, this weapon of iron and wood, and you *will* be faithful.

We run. And we sing:

> *Well, I don't know*
> *But I been told*
> *Eskimo pussy*
> *Is mighty cold. . . .*

Before chow, Sergeant Gerheim tells us that during World War I Blackjack Pershing said, "The deadliest weapon in the world is a Marine and his rifle." At Belleau Wood the Marines were so vicious that the German infantrymen called them *Teufel-Hunden*— "devil dogs."

Sergeant Gerheim explains that it is important for us to understand that it is our killer instinct which must be harnessed if we expect to survive in combat. Our rifle is only a tool; it is a hard heart that kills.

Our will to kill must be focused the way our rifle focuses a firing pressure of fifty thousand pounds per square inch to propel a piece of lead. If our rifles are not properly cleaned the explosion will be improperly focused and our rifles will shatter. If our killer instincts are not clean and strong, we will hesitate at the moment of truth. We will not kill. We will become dead Marines. And then we will be in a world of shit because Marines are not allowed to die without permission; we are government property.

The Confidence Course: We go hand over hand down a rope strung at a forty-five-degree angle across a pond—the slide-for-life. We hang upside down like monkeys and crawl headfirst down the rope.

Leonard falls off the slide-for-life eighteen times. He almost drowns. He cries. He climbs the tower. He tries again. He falls off again. This time he sinks.

Cowboy and I dive into the pond. We pull Leonard out of the muddy water. He's unconscious. When he comes to, he cries.

Back at the squad bay Sergeant Gerheim fits a Trojan rubber over the mouth of a canteen and throws the canteen at Leonard. The canteen hits Leonard on the side of the head. Sergeant Gerheim bellows, "Marines *do not* cry!"

Leonard is ordered to nurse on the canteen every day after chow.


During bayonet training Sergeant Gerheim dances an aggressive ballet. He knocks us down with a pugil stick, a five-foot pole with heavy padding on both ends. We play war with the pugil sticks. We beat each other without mercy. Then Sergeant Gerheim orders us to fix bayonets.

Sergeant Gerheim demonstrates effective attack techniques to a recruit named Barnard, a soft-spoken farm boy from Maine. The beefy drill instructor knocks out two of Private Barnard's teeth with a rifle butt.

The purpose of bayonet training, Sergeant Gerheim explains, is to awaken our killer instincts. The killer instinct will make us fearless and aggressive, like animals. If the meek ever inherit the earth the strong will take it away from them. The weak exist to be devoured by the strong. Every Marine must pack his own gear. Every Marine must be the instrument of his own salvation. It's hard, but there it is.

Private Barnard, his jaw bleeding, his mouth a bloody hole, demonstrates that he has been paying attention. Private Barnard grabs his rifle and, sitting up, bayonets Sergeant Gerheim through the right thigh.

Sergeant Gerheim grunts. Then he responds with a vertical butt stroke, but misses. So he backhands Private Barnard across the face with his fist.

Whipping off his web belt, Sergeant Gerheim ties a crude tourniquet around his bloody thigh. Then he makes the unconscious Private Barnard a squad leader. "Goddamn it, there's one little maggot who knows that the spirit of the bayonet is to *kill!* He'll make a damn fine field Marine. He ought to be a fucking general."

On the last day of our sixth week I wake up and find my rifle in my rack. My rifle is under my blanket, beside me. I don't know how it got there.

My mind isn't on my responsibilities and I forget to remind Leonard to shave.

Inspection. Junk on the bunk. Sergeant Gerheim points out that Private Pyle did not stand close enough to his razor.

Sergeant Gerheim orders Leonard and the recruit squad leaders into the head.

In the head, Sergeant Gerheim orders us to piss into a toilet bowl. "LOCK THEM HEELS! YOU ARE AT ATTENTION! READDDDDY . . . WHIZZZZ. . . ."

We whiz.

Sergeant Gerheim grabs the back of Leonard's neck and forces Leonard to his knees, pushes his head down into the yellow pool. Leonard struggles. Bubbles. Panic gives Leonard strength; Sergeant Gerheim holds him down.

After we're sure that Leonard has drowned, Sergeant Gerheim flushes the toilet. When the water stops flowing, Sergeant Gerheim releases his hold on Leonard's neck.

Sergeant Gerheim's imagination is both cruel and comprehensive, but nothing works. Leonard continues to fuck up. Now, whenever Leonard makes a mistake, Sergeant Gerheim does not punish Leonard. He punishes the whole platoon. He excludes Leonard from the punishment. While Leonard rests, we do squat-thrusts and side-straddle hops, many, many of them.

Leonard touches my arm as we move through the chow line with our metal trays. "I just can't do nothing right. I need some help. I don't want you boys to be in trouble. I—"

I move away.

The first night of our seventh week of training the platoon gives Leonard a blanket party.

Midnight.

The fire watch stands by. Private Philips, the House Mouse, Sergeant Gerheim's "go-fer," pads barefoot down the squad bay to watch for Sergeant Gerheim.

In the dark, one hundred recruits walk to Leonard's rack.

Leonard is grinning, even in his sleep.

The squad leaders hold towels and bars of soap.

Four recruits throw a blanket over Leonard. They

grip the corners of the blanket so that Leonard can't sit up and so that his screams will be muffled.

I hear the hard breathing of a hundred sweating bodies and I hear the fump and thud as Cowboy and Private Barnard beat Leonard with bars of soap slung in towels.

Leonard's screams are like the braying of a sick mule, heard far away. He struggles.

The eyes of the platoon are on me. Eyes are aimed at me in the dark, eyes like rubies.

Leonard stops screaming.

I hesitate. The eyes are on me. I step back.

Cowboy punches me in the chest with his towel and a bar of soap.

I sling the towel, drop in the soap, and then I beat Leonard, who has stopped moving. He lies in silence, stunned, gagging for air. I beat him harder and harder and when I feel tears being flung from my eyes, I beat him harder for it.


The next day, on the parade deck, Leonard does not grin.

When Gunnery Sergeant Gerheim asks, "What do we do for a living, ladies?" and we reply, "KILL! KILL! KILL!," Leonard remains silent. When our junior drill instructors ask, "Do we love the Crotch, ladies? Do we love our beloved Corps?" and the platoon responds with one voice, "GUNG HO! GUNG HO! GUNG HO!," Leonard is silent.


On the third day of our seventh week we move to the rifle range and shoot holes in paper targets. Sergeant Gerheim brags about the marksmanship of ex-Marines Charles Whitman and Lee Harvey Oswald.

By the end of our seventh week Leonard has become a model recruit. We decide that Leonard's silence is a result of his new intense concentration. Day by day, Leonard is more motivated, more squared away. His manual of arms is flawless now, but his eyes are milk glass. Leonard cleans his weapon more than any recruit in the platoon. Every night after chow Leonard caresses the scarred oak stock with linseed oil the way hundreds of earlier recruits have caressed the same piece of wood. Leonard improves at everything, but remains silent. He does what he is told but he is no longer part of the platoon.

We can see that Sergeant Gerheim resents Leonard's attitude. He reminds Leonard that the motto of the Marine Corps is *Semper Fidelis*—"Always Faithful." Sergeant Gerheim reminds Leonard that "Gung ho" is Chinese for "working together."

It is a Marine Corps tradition, Sergeant Gerheim says, that Marines never abandon their dead or wounded. Sergeant Gerheim is careful not to come down too hard on Leonard as long as Leonard remains squared away. We have already lost seven recruits on Section Eight discharges. A Kentucky boy named Perkins stepped to the center of the squad bay and slashed his wrists with his bayonet. Sergeant Gerheim was not happy to see a recruit bleeding upon his nice clean squad bay. The recruit was ordered to police the area, mop up the blood, and replace the bayonet in its sheath. While Perkins mopped up the blood, Sergeant Gerheim called a school circle and poo-pooed the recruit's shallow slash across his wrists with a bayonet. The U.S.M.C.—approved method of recruit suicide is to get *alone* and take a razor blade and slash deep and vertical, from wrist to elbow, Sergeant Gerheim said. Then he allowed Perkins to double-time to sick bay.

Sergeant Gerheim leaves Leonard alone and concentrates on the rest of us.

Sunday.

*Magic show.* Religious services in the faith of your choice—and you *will* have a choice—because religious services are specified in the beautiful full-color brochures the Crotch distributes to Mom and Dad back in hometown America, even though Sergeant Gerheim assures us that the Marine Corps was here before God. "You can give your heart to Jesus but your ass belongs to the Corps."

After the "magic show" we eat chow. The squad leaders read grace from cards set in holders on the tables. Then: "SEATS!"

We spread butter on slices of bread and then sprinkle sugar on the butter. We smuggle the sandwiches out of the mess hall, risking a beating for the novelty of unscheduled chow. We don't give a shit; we're salty. Now, when Sergeant Gerheim and his junior drill instructors stomp us we tell them that we love it and to do it some more. When Sergeant Gerheim commands: "Okay, ladies, give me fifty squatthrusts. And some side-straddle hops. Many, many of them," we laugh and then do them.

The drill instructors are proud to see that we are growing beyond their control. The Marine Corps does not want robots. The Marine Corps wants killers. The Marine Corps wants to build indestructible men, men without fear. Civilians may choose to submit or to fight back. The drill instructors leave recruits no choice. Marines fight back or they do not survive. There it is. No slack.

Graduation is only a few days away and the salty recruits of Platoon 30-92 are ready to eat their own guts and then ask for seconds. The moment the Commandant of the Marine Corps gives us the word, we will grab the Viet Cong guerrillas and the battle-hardened North Vietnamese regulars by their scrawny throats and we'll punch their fucking heads off.

Sunday afternoon in the sun. We scrub our little green garments on a long concrete table.

For the hundredth time, I tell Cowboy that I want to slip my tube steak into his sister so what will he take in trade?

For the hundredth time, Cowboy replies, "What do you have?"

Sergeant Gerheim struts around the table. He is trying not to limp. He criticizes our utilization of the Marine Corps scrub brush.

We don't care; we're too salty.

Sergeant Gerheim won the Navy Cross on Iwo Jima, he says. He got it for teaching young Marines how to bleed, he says. Marines are supposed to bleed in tidy little pools because Marines are disciplined. Civilians and members of the lesser services bleed all over the place like bed wetters.

We don't listen. We swap scuttlebutt. Laundry day is the only time we are allowed to talk to each other.

Philips—Sergeant Gerheim's black, silver-tongued House Mouse—is telling everybody about the one thousand cherries he has busted.

I say, "Leonard talks to his rifle."

A dozen recruits look up. They hesitate. Some look

sick. Others look scared. And some look shocked and angry, as though I'd just slapped a cripple.

I force myself to speak: "Leonard talks to his rifle." Nobody moves. Nobody says anything. "I don't think Leonard can hack it anymore. I think Leonard is a Section Eight."

Now guys all along the table are listening. They look confused. Their eyes seem fixed on some distant object as though they are trying to remember a bad dream.

Private Barnard nods. "I've been having this nightmare. My . . . rifle talks to me." He hesitates. "And I've been talking back to it. . . ."

"There it is," says Philips. "Yeah. Its cold. Its a cold voice. I thought I was going plain fucking crazy. My rifle said—"

Sergeant Gerheim's big fist drives Philips's next word down his throat and out of his asshole. Philips is nailed to the deck. He's on his back. His lips are crushed. He groans.

The platoon freezes.

Sergeant Gerheim puts his fists on his hips. His eyes glare out from under the brim of his Smokey the Bear campaign cover like the barrels of a shotgun. "Private Pyle is a Section Eight. You hear me? If Private Pyle talks to his piece it is because he's plain fucking crazy. You maggots *will* belay all this scuttlebutt. Don't let Private Joker play with your imaginations. I don't want to hear another word. Do you hear me? Not one word."

Night at Parris Island. We stand by until Sergeant Gerheim snaps out his last order of the day: "Prepare to mount. . . . Readddy . . . MOUNT!" Then we're lying on our backs in our skivvies, at attention, our weapons held at port arms.

We say our prayers:

*I am a United States Marine Corps recruit. I serve in the forces which guard my country and my way of life. I am prepared to give my life in their defense, so help me God . . . GUNG HO! GUNG HO! GUNG HO!*

Then the Rifleman's Creed, by Marine Corps Major General W. H. Rupertus:

*This is my rifle. There are many like it but this one is mine. My rifle is my best friend. It is my life. I must master it as I master my life.*

*My rifle, without me, is useless. I must fire my rifle true. I must shoot straighter than my enemy who is trying to kill me. I must shoot him before he shoots me.*

*I will.*

Leonard is speaking for the first time in weeks. His voice booms louder and louder. Heads turn. Bodies shift. The platoon voice fades. Leonard is about to explode. His words are being coughed up from some deep, ugly place.

Sergeant Gerheim has the night duty. He struts to Leonard's rack and stands by, fists on hips.

Leonard doesn't see Sergeant Gerheim. The veins in Leonard's neck are bulging as he bellows:

MY RIFLE IS HUMAN, EVEN AS I, BECAUSE IT IS MY LIFE. THUS I WILL LEARN IT AS A BROTHER. I WILL LEARN ITS ACCESSORIES, ITS SIGHTS, ITS BARREL.

I WILL KEEP MY RIFLE CLEAN AND READY, EVEN AS I AM CLEAN AND READY. WE WILL BECOME PART OF EACH OTHER.

WE WILL . . .

BEFORE GOD I SWEAR THIS CREED. MY RIFLE AND MYSELF ARE THE MASTER OF OUR ENEMY. WE ARE THE SAVIORS OF MY LIFE.

SO BE IT, UNTIL VICTORY IS AMERICA'S AND THERE IS NO ENEMY BUT PEACE!

AMEN.

Sergeant Gerheim kicks Leonard's rack. "Hey—*you*—Private Pyle. . . ."

"What? Yes? YES, SIR!" Leonard snaps to attention in his rack. "AYE-AYE, SIR!"

"What's that weapon's name, maggot?"

"SIR, THE PRIVATE'S WEAPON'S NAME IS CHARLENE, SIR!"

"At ease, maggot." Sergeant Gerheim grins. "You are becoming one sharp recruit, Private Pyle. Most motivated prive in my herd. Why, I may even allow you to serve as a rifleman in my beloved Corps. I had you figured for a shitbird, but you'll make a good grunt."

"AYE-AYE, SIR!"

I look at the rifle slung on my rack. It's a beautiful instrument, gracefully designed, solid and symmetrical. My rifle is clean, oiled, and works perfectly. It's a fine tool. I touch it.

Sergeant Gerheim marches down the length of the squad bay. "THE REST OF YOU ANIMALS COULD TAKE LESSONS FROM PRIVATE PYLE. He's squared away. You are all squared away. Tomorrow you will be Marines. READDDY . . . SLEEP!"

Graduation day. A thousand new Marines stand tall on the parade deck, lean and tan in immaculate khaki, their clean weapons held at port arms.

Leonard is selected as the outstanding recruit from Platoon 30-92. He is awarded a free set of dress blues and is allowed to wear the colorful uniform when the graduating platoons pass in review. The Commanding General of Parris Island shakes Leonard's hand and gives him a "Well done." Our series commander pins a RIFLE EXPERT badge on Leonard's chest and our company commander awards Leonard a citation for shooting the highest score in the training battalion.

Because of a special commendation submitted by Sergeant Gerheim, I'm promoted to Private First Class. After our series commander pins on my EXPERT'S badge, Sergeant Gerheim presents me with two red and green chevrons and explains that they're his old PFC stripes.

When we pass in review I walk right guide, tall and proud.

Cowboy receives an EXPERT's badge and is selected to carry the platoon guidon.

## THE SPIRIT OF THE BAYONET

The Commanding General of Parris Island speaks into a microphone: "Have you seen the light? The white light? The great light? The guiding light? Do you have the vision?"

And we cheer, happy beyond belief.

The Commanding General sings. We sing too:

> *Hey, Marine, have you heard?*
> *Hey, Marine. . . .*
> *L. B. J. has passed the word.*
> *Hey, Marine. . . .*
> *Say good-bye to Dad and Mom.*
> *Hey, Marine. . . .*
> *You're gonna die in Viet Nam.*
> *Hey, Marine, yeah!*

After the graduation ceremony our orders are distributed. Cowboy, Leonard, Private Barnard, Philips, and most of the other Marines in Platoon 30-92 are ordered to ITR—the Infantry Training Regiment—to be trained as grunts, infantrymen.

My orders instruct me to report to the Basic Military Journalism School at Fort Benjamin Harrison, Indiana, after I graduate from ITR. Sergeant Gerheim is disgusted by the fact that I am to be a combat correspondent and not a grunt. He calls me a poge, an office pinky. He says that shitbirds get all the slack.

Standing at ease on the parade deck, beneath the monument to the Iwo Jima flag raising, Sergeant Gerheim says, "The smoking lamp is lit. You people are no longer maggots. Today you are Marines. Once a Marine, always a Marine. . . ."

Leonard laughs out loud.

25

Our last night on the island.

I draw fire watch.

I stand by in utility trousers, skivvy shirt, spit-shined combat boots, and a helmet liner which has been painted silver.

Sergeant Gerheim gives me his wristwatch and a flashlight. "Good night, Marine."

I march up and down the squad bay between two perfectly aligned rows of racks.

One hundred young Marines breathe peacefully as they sleep—one hundred survivors from our original hundred and twenty.

Tomorrow at dawn we'll all board cattle-car buses for the ride to Camp Geiger in North Carolina. There, ITR—the infantry training regiment. All Marines are grunts, even though some of us will learn additional military skills. After advanced infantry training we'll be allowed pogey bait at the slop chute and we'll be given weekend liberty off the base and then we'll receive assignments to our permanent duty stations.

The squad bay is as quiet as a funeral parlor at midnight. The silence is disturbed only by the soft *creak-creak* of bedsprings and an occasional cough.

It's almost time for me to wake my relief when I hear a voice. Some recruit is talking in his sleep.

I stop. I listen. A second voice. Two guys must be swapping scuttlebutt. If Sergeant Gerheim hears them it'll be my ass. I hurry toward the sound.

It's Leonard. Leonard is talking to his rifle. But there is also another voice   A whisper. A cold, seductive moan. It's the voice of a woman.

Leonard's rifle is not slung on his rack. He's holding his rifle, hugging it. "Okay, okay. I *love* you!" Very softly: "I've given you the best months of my life. And now you—" I snap on my flashlight. Leonard ignores me. "I LOVE YOU! DON'T YOU UNDERSTAND? I CAN DO IT. I'LL DO ANYTHING!"

Leonards words reverberate down the squad bay. Racks squeak. Someone rolls over. One recruit sits up, rubs his eyes.

I watch the far end of the squad bay. I wait for the light to go on inside Sergeant Gerheim's palace.

I touch Leonard's shoulder. "Hey, shut your mouth, Leonard. Sergeant Gerheim will break my back."

Leonard sits up. He looks at me. He strips off his skivvy shirt and ties it around his face to blindfold himself. He begins to field-strip his weapon. "This is the first time I've ever seen her naked." He pulls off the blindfold. His fingers continue to break down the rifle into components. Then, gently, he fondles each piece. "Just look at that pretty trigger guard. Have you ever seen a more beautiful piece of metal?" He starts snapping the steel components back together. "Her connector assembly is so beautiful. . . ."

Leonard continues to babble as his trained fingers reassemble the black metal hardware.

I think about Vanessa, my girl back home. We're on a river bank, wrapped in an old sleeping bag, and I'm fucking her eyes out. But my favorite fantasy has gone stale. Thinking about Vanessa's thighs, her dark nipples, her full lips doesn't give me a hard-on anymore. I guess it must be the saltpeter in our food, like they say.

Leonard reaches under his pillow and comes out with a loaded magazine. Gently, he inserts the metal magazine into his weapon, into Charlene.

"Leonard . . . where did you get those live rounds?"

Now a lot of guys are sitting up, whispering, "What's happening?" to each other.

Sergeant Gerheim's light floods the far end of the squad bay.

"OKAY, LEONARD, LET'S GO." I'm determined to save my own ass if I can, certain that Leonard's is forfeit in any case. The last time Sergeant Gerheim caught a recruit with a live round—just one round— he ordered the recruit to dig a grave ten feet long and ten feet deep. The whole platoon had to fall out for the "funeral." I say, "You're in a world of shit now, Leonard."

The overhead lights explode. The squad bay is washed with light. "WHAT'S THIS MICKEY MOUSE SHIT? JUST WHAT IN THE NAME OF JESUS H. CHRIST ARE YOU ANIMALS DOING IN MY SQUAD BAY?"

Sergeant Gerheim comes at me like a mad dog. His voice cuts the squad bay in half: "MY BEAUTY SLEEP HAS BEEN INTERRUPTED, LADIES. YOU *KNOW* WHAT THAT MEANS. YOU HEAR ME, HERD? IT MEANS THAT ONE RECRUIT HAS VOLUNTEERED HIS YOUNG HEART FOR A GODDAMN HUMAN SACRIFICE!"

Leonard pounces from his rack, confronts Sergeant Gerheim.

Now the whole platoon is awake. We all wait to see what Sergeant Gerheim will do, confident that it will be worth watching.

"Private Joker. You shitbird. Front and center."

I move my ass. "AYE-AYE, SIR!"

"Okay, you little maggot, *speak*. Why is Private Pyle out of his rack after lights out? Why is Private

Pyle holding that weapon? Why ain't you stomping Private Pyle's guts out?"

"SIR, it is the private's duty to report to the drill instructor that Private . . . Pyle . . . has a full magazine and has locked and loaded, SIR."

Sergeant Gerheim looks at Leonard and nods. He sighs. Gunnery Sergeant Gerheim looks more than a little ridiculous in his pure white skivvies and red rubber flip-flop shower shoes and hairy legs and tattooed forearms and a beer gut and a face the color of raw beef, and, on his bald head, the green and brown Smokey the Bear campaign cover.

Our senior drill instructor focuses all of his considerable powers of intimidation into his best John-Wayne-on-Suribachi voice: "Listen to me, Private Pyle. You *will* place your weapon on your rack and—"

"NO! YOU CAN'T HAVE HER! SHE'S MINE! YOU HEAR ME? SHE'S MINE! I LOVE HER!"

Gunnery Sergeant Gerheim can't control himself any longer. "NOW YOU LISTEN TO ME, YOU FUCKING WORTHLESS LITTLE PIECE OF SHIT. YOU *WILL* GIVE ME THAT WEAPON OR I'M GOING TO TEAR YOUR BALLS OFF AND STUFF THEM DOWN YOUR SCRAWNY LITTLE THROAT! YOU HEAR ME, MARINE? I'M GOING TO PUNCH YOUR FUCKING HEART OUT!"

Leonard aims the weapon at Sergeant Gerheim's heart, caresses the trigger guard, then caresses the trigger. . . .

Sergeant Gerheim is suddenly calm. His eyes, his manner are those of a wanderer who has found his home. He is a man in complete control of himself and of the world he lives in. His face is cold and beautiful as the dark side surfaces. He smiles. It is not

29

a friendly smile, but an evil smile, as though Sergeant Gerheim were a werewolf baring its fangs. "Private Pyle, I'm proud—"

*Bang.*

The steel buttplate slams into Leonard's shoulder.

One 7.62-millimeter high-velocity copper-jacketed bullet punches Gunnery Sergeant Gerheim back.

He falls.

We all stare at Sergeant Gerheim. Nobody moves.

Sergeant Gerheim sits up as though nothing has happened. For one second, we relax. Leonard has missed. Then dark blood squirts from a little hole in Sergeant Gerheim's chest. The red blood blossoms into his white skivvy shirt like a beautiful flower. Sergeant Gerheim's bug eyes are focused upon the blood rose on his chest, fascinated. He looks up at Leonard. He squints. Then he relaxes. The werewolf smile is frozen on his lips.

My menial position of authority as the fire watch on duty forces me to act. "Now, uh, Leonard, we're all your bros, man, your brothers. I'm your bunkmate, right? I—"

"Sure," says Cowboy. "Go easy, Leonard. We don't want to hurt you."

"Affirmative," says Private Barnard.

Leonard doesn't hear. "Did you see the way he looked at her? Did you? I knew what he was thinking. I knew. That fat pig and his dirty—"

"Leonard. . . ."

"We can kill you. You know that." Leonard caresses his rifle. "Don't you know that Charlene and I can kill you all?"

Leonard aims his rifle at my face.

I don't look at the rifle. I look into Leonard's eyes. I know that Leonard is too weak to control his instrument of death. It is a hard heart that kills, not the weapon. Leonard is a defective instrument for the power that is flowing through him. Sergeant Gerheim's mistake was in not seeing that Leonard was like a glass rifle which would shatter when fired. Leonard is not hard enough to harness the power of an interior explosion to propel the cold black bullet of his will.

Leonard is grinning at us, the final grin that is on the face of death, the terrible grin of the skull.

The grin changes to a look of surprise and then to confusion and then to terror as Leonard's weapon moves up and back and then Leonard takes the black metal barrel into his mouth. "NO! Not—"

*Bang.*

Leonard is dead on the deck. His head is now an awful lump of blood and facial bones and sinus fluids and uprooted teeth and jagged, torn flesh. The skin looks plastic and unreal.

The civilians will demand yet another investigation, of course. But during the investigation the recruits of Platoon 30-92 will testify that Private Pratt, while highly motivated, was a ten percenter who did not pack the gear to be a Marine in our beloved Corps.

Sergeant Gerheim is still smiling. He was a fine drill instructor. Dying, that's what we're here for, he would have said—blood makes the grass grow. If he could speak, Gunnery Sergeant Gerheim would explain to Leonard why the guns that we love don't love back. And he would say, "Well done."

I turn off the overhead lights.

I say, "Prepare to mount." Then: "MOUNT!"

The platoon falls into a hundred racks.

I feel cold and alone. I am not alone. All over Parris Island there are thousands and thousands of us. And, all around the world, hundreds of thousands.

I try to sleep. . . .

In my rack, I pull my rifle into my arms. She talks to me. Words come out of the wood and metal and flow into my hands. She tells me what to do.

My rifle is a solid instrument of death. My rifle is black steel. Our human bodies are bags of blood, easy to puncture and quick to drain, but our hard tools of death cannot be broken.

I hold my weapon at port arms, gently, as though she were a holy relic, a magic wand wrought with interlocking pieces of silver and iron, with a teak-wood stock, golden bullets, a crystal bolt, jewels to sight with. My weapon obeys me. I'll hold Vanessa, my rifle. I'll hold her. I'll just hold her for a little while. I will hide in this dark dream for as long as I can.

Blood pours out of the barrel of my rifle and flows up on to my hands. The blood moves. The blood breaks up into living fragments. Each fragment is a spider. Millions and millions of tiny red spiders of blood are crawling up my arms, across my face, into my mouth. . . .

Silence. In the dark, a hundred men are breathing in unison.

I look at Cowboy, then at Private Barnard. They understand. Cold grins of death are frozen on their faces. They nod.

The newly minted Marines in my platoon stand to

32

attention, horizontal in their racks, their weapons at port arms.

The Marines wait, a hundred young werewolves with guns in their hands.

I lead:

*This is my rifle.*
*There are many like it, but this one is mine. . . .*

# BODY COUNT

*I saw the best minds of my generation destroyed by madness, starving hysterical naked . . .*

—ALLEN GINSBERG, *Howl*

*A psychotic is a guy who's just found out what's going on.*

—WILLIAM S. BURROUGHS

Tet: The Year of the Monkey.

Rafter Man and I spend the Vietnamese lunar New Year's Eve, 1968, at the Freedom Hill PX near Da Nang. I've been ordered to write a feature article on the Freedom Hill Recreation Center on Hill 327 for *Leatherneck* magazine. I'm a combat correspondent assigned to the First Marine Division. My job is to write upbeat news features which are distributed to the highly paid civilian news correspondents who shack up with their Eurasian maids in big hotels in Da Nang. The ten correspondents in the First Division's Informational Services Office are reluctant public relations men for the war in general and for the Marine Corps in particular. This morning my commanding officer decided that a really inspiring piece could be written about Hill 327, an angle being the fact that Hill 327 was the first permanent position occupied by American forces. Major Lynch thinks I rate some slack before I return to the ISO office in Phu Bai. My last three field operations were real shitkickers; in the field, a Marine correspondent is just another rifleman. Rafter Man tags along behind me like a kid. Rafter Man is a combat photographer. He has never been in the shit. He thinks I'm one hard field Marine.

We go into a movie theater that looks like a warehouse and we watch John Wayne in *The Green Berets*, a Hollywood soap opera about the love of guns. We sit way down front, near some grunts. The grunts are sprawled across their seats and they've propped muddy jungle boots onto the seats in front of them. They are bearded, dirty, out of uniform, and look lean and mean, the way human beings look after they've survived a long hump in the jungle, the boonies, the bad bush.

I prop my boots on the seats and we watch John Wayne leading the Green Beanies. John Wayne is a beautiful soldier, clean-shaven, sharply attired in tailored tiger-stripe jungle utilities, wearing boots that shine like black glass. Inspired by John Wayne, the fighting soldiers from the sky go hand-to-hand with all of the Victor Charlies in Southeast Asia. He snaps out an order to an Oriental actor who played Mr. Sulu on "Star Trek." Mr. Sulu, now playing an Arvin officer, delivers a line with great conviction: "First *kill* . . . all stinking Cong . . . then go home." The audience of Marines roars with laughter. This is the funniest movie we have seen in a long time.

Later, at the end of the movie, John Wayne walks off into the sunset with a spunky little orphan. The grunts laugh and whistle and threaten to pee all over themselves. The sun is setting in the South China Sea—in the East—which makes the end of the movie as accurate as the rest of it.

Most of the zoomies in the audience are clean-shaven office poges who never go into the field. The poges wear spit-shined boots and starched utilities and Air Force sunglasses. The poges stare at the grunts as though the grunts were Hell's Angels at the ballet.

After the screen loses its color and the overhead lights come on, one of the poges says, "Fucking grunts . . . they're nothing but animals. . . ."

The grunts turn around. One grunt stands up. He walks over to where the poges are sitting.

The poges laugh and punch each other and mock the grunt's angry face. Then they are silent. They stare at the grunt's face. He's smiling now. He's smiling like a man who knows a terrible secret.

The zoomie poges do not ask the grunt to explain why he is smiling. They don't want to know.

Another grunt jumps up, punches the smiling grunt on the arm, says, "Hey, fuck it, Mother. It ain't no big thing. We don't want to waste these assholes."

The smiling Marine takes a step forward, but the smaller man stands in his path.

The poges take advantage of the smiling grunt's delay. They walk backwards up the aisle until they reach the door, then stumble out into sunlight.

I say, "Well, no shit. And they say grunts are killers. You ladies do not look like killers to me."

The smiling grunt is not smiling anymore. He says, "Okay, you son-of-a-bitch. . . ."

"Stand by, Mother," says the small Marine. "I know this shitbird."

Cowboy and I grab each other and wrestle and punch and pound each other on the back. We say, "Hey, you old mother-fucker. How you been? What's happening? Been getting any? Only your sister. Well, better my sister than my mom, although mom's not bad."

"Hey, Joker, I was hoping I'd never see you again, you piece of shit. I was hoping that Gunny Gerheim's ghost would keep you on Parris Island for-*ev*-er and that he would *give* you motivation."

I laugh. "Cowboy, you shitbird. You look real mean. If I didn't know that you're a born poge I'd be scared."

Cowboy grunts. "This is Animal Mother. He *is* mean."

The big Marine is picking his nose. "You better motherfucking believe it." A belt of machine-gun bullets crisscross the Marine's chest so that he looks like a big Mexican bandit.

I say, "This is Rafter Man. He's not a walking camera store. He's a photographer."

"You a photographer?"

I shake my head. "I'm a combat correspondent."

Animal Mother sneers, exposing rotten canine teeth. "You seen much 'combat'?

"Hey, don't give me any shit, asshole. My payback is a motherfucker. I got twice as many operations as any grunt in Eye Corps. I'm just scarfing up some bennies. My office is up in Phu Bai."

"Yeah?" Cowboy punches me in the chest. "That's our area. One-Five. Delta Company—the baddest of the bad, the leanest of the lean, the meanest of the mean. We hitched down here this morning. We rate some slack 'cause our squad wasted beaucoup Victor Charlies. Man, we are life takers and heartbreakers. Just ask for the Lusthog Squad, first platoon. We shoot them full of holes, bro. We fill them full of lead."

I grin. "Sergeant Gerheim would be proud to hear it."

"Yeah," Cowboy says, nodding his head. "Yeah, I guess so." He looks away. "I hate Viet Nam. They don't even have horses here. Why, there's not one horse in all of Viet Nam."

Cowboy turns away and introduces us to his squad: Alice, a black man as big as Animal Mother; Donlon, the radioman; Lance Corporal Stutten, honcho of the third fire team; Doc Jay, the squad's Navy corpsman; T.H.E. Rock; and the leader of the Lusthog Squad, Crazy Earl.

Crazy Earl is carrying an M-16 Colt automatic rifle slung on his shoulder, but in his hands is a Red Ryder BB gun. He's as skinny as a death-camp survivor, and his face consists of a long, pointed nose with a hollow cheek on each side. His eyes are magnified by thick lenses and one arm of his gray Marine-issue eyeglasses has been wired back on with too much wire. He says, "Saddle up," and the grunts start picking up their gear, their M-16's and M-79 grenade launchers and captured AK-47 assault rifles, their ruck-sacks, flak jackets, and helmets. Animal Mother picks up an M-60 machine gun and sets the butt into his hip so that the black barrel slants up at a forty-five-degree angle. Animal Mother grunts. Crazy Earl turns to Cowboy and says, "We better be moving, bro. Mr. Shortround will punch our hearts out if we're late."

Cowboy is picking up his gear. "That's affirmative, Craze. But you got to talk to Joker, man. We were on the island together. He'll write you up and make you famous."

Crazy Earl looks at me. There is no expression on his face. "There it is. They call me Crazy Earl. Gooks love me until I blow them away. Then they don't love me anymore."

I grin. "There it is."

Crazy Earl grins, gives me a thumbs-up, says, "Moving, Cowboy," and then leads his squad out of the theater.

Cowboy punches me on the shoulder. "That's my fearless leader, bro. I'm the first fire-team leader. I'll be squad leader soon. I'm just waiting for Craze to get wasted. Or maybe he'll just go plain fucking crazy. That's how Craze got to be honcho. Ol' Stoke, he was our honcho before Craze. Ol' Supergrunt. Went stark raving. Pretty soon it'll be my turn."

"Hey, you keep your shit together, Cowboy. You know you're a fool. You know you can't take care of yourself. Remember how easy it was for me to zap you when Sergeant Gerheim made me play sniper? I mean, the Crotch ought to fly your mom over here so that she can go into the bush with you."

Cowboy takes a few steps toward the door, turns, waves goodbye, grins.

I give him the finger.

After Cowboy and his squad are gone, Rafter Man and I watch a "Pink Panther" cartoon. Then we pick up our weapons and head for the PX, which looks like another warehouse. We buy junk food; pogey bait.

As we wait to pay for our pogey bait with military payment certificates, Rafter Man tries to find some words. "Joker, I want . . . I want to go out. I want to go out into the field. I been in country for almost three months. Three *months*. All I do is take hand-shake shots at award ceremonies. That's number ten, the worst. I'm bored. A high-school girl could do my job." He gives MPC's to a pretty Vietnamese cashier.

Outside, an apprentice Viet Cong forces me to submit to a boot shine while his older sister exhibits her breasts to Rafter Man.

"Relax, Rafter. You owe it to yourself. You'll be in the field soon enough."

"Come on, Joker, cut me a huss. How can I teach geography if I never see the world? Take me to Phu Bai. Okay?"

"Right," I say. "And then you'll get yourself wasted the first day you're in the field and it'll be my fault. Your mom will find me after I rotate back to the World. Your mom will beat the shit out of me. That's a negative, Rafter. I'm not a sergeant, I'm only a corporal. I'm not responsible for your scrawny little ass."

"Yes you are. I'm only a lance corporal."

Rafter Man and I stop by the USO and exchange a few off-color jokes with the round-eyed Red Cross girls, who give us donuts. We ask the Red Cross girls if they expect us to satisfy our lust with a donut and they explain that a donut hole is all we rate.

In the USO there are barrels and barrels of letters which have been written to us by children back in the World:

Dear Soldiers in Red Alert:
We have learned that men in Vietnam alive or dead are the bravest. We are all trying to help you all to come home to your house. We'll buy bonds.

We help the Red Cross to help soldiers. We'll help you and your allies to come back. If possible, we'll send you gifts.

> From Your Country,
> Cheri

Dear Friend in Battle:

I am eight years old. I have one brother. I have one sister. It must be sad over there.

> Sincerely,
> Jeff

Dear American:

I wish I could see you instead of talking on this Card. We have a dog, and it is so cute. It is black and has long hair. My name is Lori. I will always remember you in my prayers. Tell everyone I love them and I love you too, so good-bye.

> Your Friend,
> Lori

Rafter Man reads the letters out loud. He can still be touched by them.

To me, the letters are like shoes for the dead, who do not walk.

As dusk approaches, Rafter Man and I hitchhike back to the ISO hootch in the First Marine Division HQ area.

Rafter Man writes a letter to his mother.

I take my black Magic Marker and I make a thick X over the number 59 on the shapely thigh of the life-sized nude woman I've drawn on the plywood partition behind my rack. There is a smaller version of the same woman on the back of my flak jacket.

Almost every Marine in Viet Nam carries a short-timer's calendar of his tour of duty—the usual 365 days—plus a bonus of 20 days for being a Marine. Some are drawn on flak jackets with Magic Markers. Some are drawn on helmets. Some are tattoos. Others are mimeographed drawings of Snoopy, his beagle body cut up by pale blue ink, or a helmet on a pair of boots—"The Short-Timer." The designs vary, but the most popular design is a big-busted woman-child cut up into pieces like a puzzle. Each day another fragment of her delicious anatomy is inked out, her crotch being reserved, of course, for those last few days in country.

Sitting on my rack, I type out my story about Hill 327, the serviceman's oasis, about how all of us fine young American boys are assured our daily ration of pogey bait and about how those of us who are lucky enough to visit the rear areas get to see Mr. John Wayne karate-chop Victor Charlie to death in a Technicolor cartoon about some other Viet Nam.

The article I actually write is a masterpiece. It takes talent to convince people that war is a beautiful experience. Come one, come all to exotic Viet Nam, the jewel of Southeast Asia, meet interesting, stimulating people of an ancient culture . . . and kill them. Be the first kid on your block to get a confirmed kill.

I fall into my rack. I try to sleep.

The setting sun pours orange across the rice paddies beyond our wire.

Midnight. Down in Dogpatch, in the ville, the gooks are shooting off fireworks to celebrate the Vietnamese New Year. Rafter Man and I sit on the tin roof of our hootch so that we can watch the more impressive fireworks on the Da Nang airfield. One hundred-and-twenty-two-millimeter rockets are falling from the dark sky. I open a B-3 unit and we eat John Wayne cookies, dipping them in pineapple jam.

Chewing, Rafter Man says, "I thought this was supposed to be a truce on account of Tet is their big holiday."

I shrug. "Well, I guess it's hard not to shoot somebody you've been trying to shoot for a long time just because it's a holiday."

A sudden *swooosssh*. . . .

Incoming.

I jump off the roof.

Rafter Man stands up, his mouth open. He looks down at me like I'm crazy. "What—"

A rocket hits the deck fifty yards away.

Rafter Man falls off the roof.

I jerk Rafter Man to his feet. I shove him. He falls into a sandbagged bunker.

All around the hill orange machine-gun tracers flash up into the sky. Outgoing mortars. Outgoing artillery. Incoming rockets. All kinds of noise. Illumination rounds pop high above the rice paddies. The flares sway down, glowing, suspended beneath little parachutes.

I listen for a few moments and then I grab Rafter Man and I pull him into our hootch. "Get your piece."

I pick up my M-16. I snap in a magazine. I throw a bandolier of full magazines to Rafter Man. "Lock and load, recruit. Lock and load."

"But that's against regulations."

"Do it."

Outside, headquarters personnel from the surrounding hootches are stumbling into rifle pits on the perimeter. They crouch down in the damp holes in their skivvies. They stare out through the wire.

Down on the airfield in Da Nang Victor Charlie's rockets are raining down on the concrete corrals where the Marine Air Wing parks its F-4 Phantom fighter bombers. The rockets blink like flashbulbs. The flashbulbs pop. And then the sound of drums.

The Informational Services Office on the hill is a carnival with green performers—many, many of them. The lifers are all being fearless leaders. The New Guys are about to wet their pants. Everyone is talking. Everyone is pacing and looking, pacing and looking. Most of these guys have never been in the shit. Violence doesn't excite them the way it excites me because they don't understand it the way I do. They're afraid. Death is not yet their friend. So they don't know what they're supposed to say. They don't know what they're expected to do.

Major Lynch, our commanding officer, marches in and squares us away. He tells us that Victor Charlie has used the Tet holiday to launch an offensive all over Viet Nam. Every major military target in Viet Nam has been hit. In Saigon, the United States Embassy has been overrun by suicide squads. Khe Sanh is standing by to be overrun, a second Dien Bien Phu. The term "secure area" no longer has any meaning. Only fifty yards up the hill, near the commanding general's private quarters, a Viet Cong sapper squad has blown apart a communications center with a satchel charge. Our "defeated" enemy is lashing out with a power that is shocking.

Everybody starts talking at once.

Major Lynch is calm. He stands in the center of chaos and tries to give us orders. Nobody listens. He makes us listen. His words snap out like bullets from a machine gun. "Zip up those flak jackets. Put on that helmet, Marine. Load your weapons but *do not* put a round in the chamber. Everybody *will* shut the fuck up. Joker!"

"Aye-aye, sir."

Major Lynch stands in front of the Marine Corps flag—blood red, with an eagle, globe, and anchor of gold, U.S.M.C. and SEMPER FIDELIS. He taps my chest with his finger. "Joker, you *will* take off that damned button. How is it going to look if you get killed wearing a peace symbol?"

"Aye-aye, sir!"

"Get up to Phu Bai. Captain January will need all his people."

Rafter Man steps forward. "Sir? Could I go with Joker?"

"What? Sound off."

"I'm Compton, sir. Lance Corporal Compton. From Photo. I want to get into the shit."

"Permission granted. And welcome aboard." The major turns, starts yelling at the New Guys.

I say, "Sir, I don't think that—"

Major Lynch turns back to me, irritated. "You still here? Vanish, Joker, most ricky-tick. And take the New Guy with you. You're responsible for him." The major turns away and starts snapping out orders for the defense of the First Marine Division's Informational Services Office.

Chaos at the Da Nang airfield; enemy rockets have wasted hootches, Marines, and Phantom jets. I talk to a poge in thick glasses. The poge is reading a comic book. By using my voice as an instrument of command I convince the poge that I'm an officer and that I'm on a personal errand for the Commandant of the Marine Corps. Rafter Man and I are given a priority rating and have to wait only nine hours before we're stuffed into the cavernous belly of a C-130 Hercules cargo plane with a hundred Marine Corps lifers.

Thousands of feet below, Viet Nam is a narrow strip of dried dragon shit upon which God has sprinkled toy tanks and airplanes and a lot of trees, flies, and Marines.

As we descend for a landing at Phu Bai Combat Base, Rafter Man hugs his three black-body Nikons like metal babies.

I laugh. "When the grunts see that the famous Rafter Man is here, they'll just know that the war must be over."

Rafter Man grins.

Rafter Man won his nickname the night he fell out of the rafters at the Thunderbird Club, the enlisted men's slop chute back in the First Marine Division headquarters area. An Australian comedian and two fat Korean belly dancers were entertaining an SRO audience. Rafter Man was hammered, but so was I, so I couldn't stop him. We were back near the entrance and Rafter Man decided that the only way he was going to get a good look at the seminude belly dancers was to climb up into the rafters and crawl out above the mass of green Marines.

General Motors and his staff had stopped by to catch the show. They did that sometimes. General Motors liked to keep in touch with his Marines.

Rafter Man fell off the rafters like a green bomb, crashing through the general's table, spilling beer, smashing pretzels, and knocking the general and four of his staff officers on their brass behinds.

Hundreds of enlisted men, having assumed that Rafter Man was some kind of unconventional mortar round, were one mass of green laundry. Then heads began to pop up.

The staff officers jerked Rafter Man to his feet and started yelling for the M.P.'s.

General Motors raised his hand and there was silence. Unlike many Marine Corps generals, General Motors looked exactly like a Marine Corps general, eyes as gray as gun metal, a face that was tough but sensitive—a Cro-Magnon holy man's face. His jungle utilities were starched, razor-creased, with shirtsleeves rolled up neatly.

Rafter Man stood there, staring at the general, grinning like a goddamn fool. He wobbled. He tried to walk but he couldn't. He was having enough trouble just standing in one place.

General Motors ordered the broken table cleared away. Then he offered Rafter Man his chair.

Rafter Man hesitated, looked at the general, then at the staff officers, who were still pissed off, then at me, then he looked at the general again. He grinned and sat down on the metal folding chair.

The general nodded, then sat down on the floor next to Rafter Man. With a wave of his hand he ordered the staff officers to sit on the floor behind him, which they did, still pissed off.

With another wave of his hand the general ordered the performers to go on with the show.

The Australian comedian and the sweating belly dancers hesitated.

Rafter Man stood up.

He wobbled, then sank down to the deck beside the general. He put his arm around the general's shoulders. General Motors looked at him without expression. Rafter Man said, "Hey, bro, I can fly. Did you see me fly?" He paused. "You think . . . am I drunk? I mean, am I hammered or am I hammered?" He looked around. "Joker? Where's Joker?" But I was still stumbling over angry poges. "Joker's my bro, sir. We enlisted personnel are tight, you know? Indubitably. I am in love with those sexy women. I roger that. . . ." His face got serious. "Who'll take me through the wire? Sir? Where's Joker?" He looked around, but didn't see me. "I'll fall in the wire. Or blow myself up. Sir? SIR? I'll step on a mine. I got to find my bro, sir. I don't want to fall into the wire, not again. JOKER!"

General Motors looked at Rafter Man and smiled. "Don't worry, son. Marines never abandon their wounded."

Rafter Man looked at the general the way drunks look at people who say things they don't understand. Then he smiled. He nodded. "Aye-aye, sir."

The Australian comedian and the meaty belly dancers resumed their act, which consisted primarily of double-takes from the comedian every time one of the belly dancers slung a big tender breast out of her tiny golden costume. The act was a smashing success.

By the time the show was over, Rafter Man could stand only if he had a wall to hold onto. General Motors took Rafter Man's arm and put it over his shoulders and helped Rafter Man out of the E.M. club and, leaving the staff officers behind, helped Rafter Man to stagger down the hill, along the narrow path through the tangle-foot and the concertina wire.

As the enlisted men left the Thunderbird Club, they watched this small event and they smiled and nodded and said, "Decent. Number one."

And: "There it is."


Now the C-130 Hercules propjet is taxiing to a stop. The heavy cargo door drops and slams into the runway. Rafter Man and I hop out with our fellow passengers.

There are three damaged C-130's pushed together on the port side of the airfield. On the starboard side of the airfield is the gutted carcass of another C-130, charred, still smoking. Men in tinfoil spacesuits are squirting the torn metal with white foam.

Rafter Man and I ditty-bop off the airfield and we hump down a freshly oiled dirt road until we come to the perimeter of Phu Bai Combat Base, about a mile from the airfield and thirty-four miles from the DMZ.

Phu Bai is a vast mud puddle cut into sections by perfectly aligned rows of frame hootches. The largest structure at Phu Bai is HQ for the Third Marine Division. The big wooden building stands as a symbol of our power and as a temple for those who love the power.

We stop at the guard bunker. A big dumb M.P. orders us to clear our weapons. I click the magazine out of my M-16. Rafter Man does the same. I stare back at the big dumb M.P. to assert my principles. He is scribbling on a clipboard with a stubby yellow pencil.

Suddenly the M.P. punches Rafter Man in the chest with his walnut baton. "You a New Guy?" Rafter Man nods. "I got a working party for you. You're going to fill sandbags for my bunker." The M.P. hooks his thumb toward the guard bunker in the center of the road. A big bite has been taken out of the bunker. A mortar shell has blasted through one layer of sandbags and has split open a second layer, spilling sand.

I say, "He's with me."

Sneering, the sergeant draws himself up inside his crisp, clean stateside utilities, his white helmet liner with *Military Police* stenciled in red, his white rifle belt with its gold buckle bearing the eagle, globe and anchor, his shiny new forty-five automatic pistol, and his black spit-shined stateside boots. The big dumb M.P. is smugly enthroned in his power to exact the trivial. "He'll do what *I* say, motherfucker. *Cor*poral." He thumps his black metal collar chevrons with the tip of his walnut baton. "I'm a sergeant."

I nod. "Affirmative. That's affirmative, you fucking lifer. But this man is only a lance corporal. And he takes his orders from *me*."

The big dumb M.P. shrugs. "Okay. Okay, motherfucker. You can tell *him* what to do. *You* can fill my sandbags, *cor*poral. Many, many of them."

I look at the deck. An explosion is building up inside me. I experience fear, and a terrible strain, as the pressure grows and grows, and then release, relief. "No, you dumb redneck. Negative, you fucking pig. No, I'm not going to fall out for any Mickey Mouse working party. You know why? Huh?" I slam the magazine back into my M-16 and I snap the bolt, chambering a round.

I'm smiling now. I'm smiling as I jam the flash suppressor into the big dumb M.P.'s jelly belly and then I wait for him to make one sound, any sound, or just the slightest movement and then I'm going to pull the trigger.

The big dumb M.P.'s mouth falls open. He doesn't have anything else to say. I don't think he wants me to fill his sandbags anymore.

The clipboard and the pencil fall.

Then, walking backward, the big dumb M.P. retreats into his bunker, mouth open, hands up.

Rafter Man is too scared to say anything for a while. I say, "You'll get used to this place. You'll change. You'll understand."

Rafter Man remains quiet. We walk. Then, "You weren't bluffing. You would have killed that guy. For nothing."

I say, "There it is."

Rafter Man is looking at me as though he's seeing something new. "Is everybody like that? I mean, you were laughing. Like . . ."

"It's not the kind of thing you can talk about. There's no way to explain stuff like that. After you've been in the shit, after you've got your first confirmed kill, you'll understand."

Rafter Man is silent. His questions are silent.

"At ease," I say. "Don't kid yourself, Rafter Man, this is a slaughter. In this world of shit you won't have time to understand. What you do, you become. You better learn to flow with it. You owe it to yourself."

Rafter Man nods, but he doesn't reply. I know how he feels.

The Informational Services Office for Task Force X-Ray, a unit assigned to cover elements of the First Division temporarily operating in the Third Division's area, is a small frame hootch, constructed with two-by-fours and slave labor. Nailed to the screen door is a red sign with yellow letters: TFX-ISO. Roofed with sheets of galvanized tin and walled with fine-mesh screening, the hootch is designed to protect us from the heat. The Seabees have nailed green plastic ponchos along the side of the hootch. These dusty flaps are rolled up during the furnace of the day and are rolled down at night to keep out the fierce monsoon rain.

Chili Vendor and Daytona Dave are doing fleetniks in front of the ISO hootch. Chili Vendor is a tough Chicano from East L.A. and Daytona Dave is an easygoing surf bum from a wealthy family in Florida. They have absolutely nothing in common. They are the best of friends.

About a hundred grunts have stuffed themselves into every available piece of shade in the area. Each grunt has been given a fleetnik, a printed form with spaces for all the necessary biographical data required to send a photograph of the grunt to his hometown newspaper.

Daytona Dave is taking the photographs with a black-body Nikon while Chili Vendor says, "Smile, scumbag. Say, 'shit.' Next."

The grunt next in line kneels down beside a little Vietnamese orphan of undetermined sex. Chili Vendor slaps a rubber Hershey bar into the grunt's hand. "Smile, scumbag. Say, 'shit.' Next."

Daytona Dave snaps the picture.

Chili Vendor snatches the grunt's fleetnik with one hand and the rubber Hershey bar with the other. "Next!"

The orphan says, "Hey, Marine number one! You! You! You give me chop-chop? You souvenir me?" The orphan grabs at the Hershey bar and jerks it out of Chili Vendor's hand. He bites the Hershey bar; it's rubber. He tries to tear off the wrapper; he can't. "Chop-chop number ten!"

Chili Vendor snatches the rubber Hershey bar out of the orphan's hands and tosses it to the next grunt in the line. "Keep moving. Don't you guys want to be famous? Some of you dudes probably wasted this kid's family, but back in your hometown you gonna be the big strong Marine with a heart of gold."

I say in my John Wayne voice: "Listen up, pilgrim. You skating again?"

Chili Vendor turns, sees me and grins. "Hey, Joker, qué pasa? This might be skating, man, it fucking might be. These gook orphans are hard-core. I think half of them are Viet Cong Marines."

The orphan is walking away, grumbling, kicking the road. Then, as though to prove Chili Vendor's point, the orphan pauses. He turns around and gives us the finger with both hands. Then he walks on.

Daytona Dave laughs. "That kid runs an NVA rifle company. Somebody blow him away."

I grin. "You ladies are doing an outstanding job. You're both born poges."

Chili Vendor shrugs. "Hey, bro, the Crotch don't send beaners into the field. We're too tough. We make the grunts look bad."

You guys getting hit?"

"That's affirmative," says Daytona Dave. "Every night. A few rounds. They're just fucking with us. Of course, I've got so many confirmed kills I lost count. Nobody believes me because the gooks drag off their dead. I do believe that those little yellow enemy folks eat their casualties. Blood trails all over the place, but no confirmed kills. So here I am, a hero, and Captain January has got me doing Mickey Mouse shit with this uppity wetback."

"CORPORAL JOKER!"

"SIR! Later, people. Come on, Rafter."

Chili Vendor punches Daytona Dave in the chest. "Doubletime up to the ville and souvenir me one cute orphan, man, but be sure you get a dirty one, a really skuzzy one."

"JOKER!"

"AYE-AYE, SIR!"

Captain January is in his plywood cubicle in the back of the ISO hootch. Captain January is the kind of officer who chews an unlit pipe because he thinks that a pipe will help to make him a father figure. He's playing cut-throat Monopoly with Mr. Payback. He's playing cut-throat Monopoly with Mr. Payback. snuffy in our unit. Captain January isn't Captain

57

Queeg, but then he's not Humphrey Bogart, either. He picks up his little silver shoe and moves it to Baltic Avenue, tapping each property along the way.

"I'll buy Baltic. And two houses." Captain January reaches for the white and purple deed to Baltic Avenue. "That's another monopoly, Sergeant." He positions tiny green houses on the board. "Joker, you've scarfed up beaucoup slack in Da Nang and I am sure that now you are squared away to get back into the field. Hump up to Hue. The NVA have overrun the city. One-One is in the shit."

I hesitate. "Sir, would the Captain happen to know who killed my story on that howitzer crew who wasted a whole squad of NVA with one beehive round? In Da Nang some poges told me that a colonel shit-canned my story. Some colonel said that beehive rounds were a figment of my imagination because the Geneva Convention classified them as 'inhumane' and American fighting men are incapable of being inhumane."

Mr. Payback grunts. "Inhumane? That's a pretty word for it. Ten thousand feathered stainless steel darts. Those fléchette canisters do convert gooks into lumps of shitty rags. There it is."

"Oh, *damn*," says Captain January. He slaps a card onto the field desk. "Go to jail—go directly to jail—do not pass go—do not collect two hundred dollars." The captain puts his little silver shoe into jail. "I know who killed your beehive story, Joker. What I don't know is who has been tipping off hostile reporters every time we get an adverse incident—like that white Victor Charlie recon wasted last week, the one the snuffies call 'The Phantom Blooper'. General Motors is ready

58

to bust me down to a grunt because of that leak in our security. You talk; I'll talk. Do we have a deal?"

"No. No, Captain. It's not important."

"Number one! Snake eyes! No sweat, Joker. I've got a big piece of slack for you." Captain January picks up a manila guard mail envelope and pulls out a piece of paper with fancy writing on it. "Congratulations, Sergeant Joker." He hands me the paper.

TO ALL WHO SHALL SEE THESE PRESENTS, GREETING: KNOW YE THAT REPOSING SPECIAL TRUST AND CONFIDENCE IN THE FIDELITY OF JAMES T. DAVIS, 2306777/ 4312, I DO APPOINT HIM A SERGEANT IN THE UNITED STATES MARINE CORPS. . . .

I stare at the piece of paper. Then I put the order on Captain January's field desk. "Number ten. I mean, no way, sir."

Captain January stops his little silver shoe in midstride. "What did you say, Sergeant?"

"Sir, I rose by sheer military genius to the rank of corporal, as they say, like Hitler and Napoleon. But I'm not a sergeant. I guess I'm just a snuffy at heart."

"Sergeant Joker, you *will* belay the Mickey Mouse shit. You won a meritorious promotion on Parris Island. You've got an excellent record in country. You've got enough time-in-grade. You rate this promotion. This is the only war we've got, Sergeant. Your career as a Marine—"

"*No*, sir. We bomb these people, then we photograph them. My stories are paper bullets fired into the fat black heart of Communism. I've fought to make the world safe for hypocrisy. We have met the enemy and he is us. War is good business—invest your son. Viet Nam means never having to say you're sorry. *Arbeit Macht Frei*—"

"Sergeant Joker!"

"Negative, Captain. Number ten. I'm a *cor*poral. You can send me to the brig, sir—I know that. Lock me up in Portsmouth Naval Prison until I rot, but let me rot as a corporal, sir. You know I do my job. I write that the Nam is an Asian Eldorado populated by a cute, primitive but determined people. War is a noisy breakfast food. War is fun to eat. War can give you better checkups. War cures cancer—permanently. I don't kill. I write. Grunts kill; I only watch. I'm only young Dr. Goebbels. I'm *not* a sergeant." I add: "Sir."

Captain January's silver shoe lands on Oriental Avenue. There is a tiny red plastic hotel on Oriental Avenue. Captain January grimaces and then counts out thirty-five dollars in MPC. He hands Mr. Payback the small colorful bills and then hands him the dice. "Sergeant, you *will* be wearing chevrons indicating your proper rank the next time I see you or I will definitely jump on your program. Do you want to be a grunt? If not, you *will* remove that unauthorized peace button from your duty uniform."

I don't say anything.

Captain January looks at Rafter Man. "Who's this? Sound off, Marine."

Rafter Man stutters.

I say, "This is Lance Corporal Compton, sir. The New Guy in Photo."

"Outstanding. Welcome aboard, Marine. Joker, make sleeping sounds here tonight and head up to Hue in the morning. Walter Cronkite is due here tomorrow so we'll be busy. I'll need Chili Vendor and Daytona here. But your job is important, too. General Motors called me about this personally. We need some good, clear photographs. And some hard-hitting captions. Get me photographs of indigenous civilian personnel who have been executed with their hands tied behind their backs, people buried alive, priests with their throats cut, dead babies—you know what I want. Get me some good body counts. And don't forget to calculate your kill ratios. And Joker. . . ."

"Yes, sir?"

"Don't *even* photograph any naked bodies unless they're mutilated."

"Aye-aye, sir."

"And Joker . . ."

"Yes, sir?"

"Get a haircut."

"Aye-aye, sir."

As Mr. Payback releases his little silver car Captain January says, "Three houses! Three houses! Park fucking Place! That's . . . eighty dollars!"

Mr. Payback counts out all of his money. "That breaks me, Captain. I owe you seven bucks."

Captain January rakes up the pile of MPC, a shit-eating grin on his face. "You do not understand business, Mr. Payback. If we had Marine generals who understood business this war would be over. The secret to winning this war is in public relations. Harry S Truman once said that the Marine Corps has a propaganda machine almost equal to Stalin's. He was right. In war, truth is the first casualty. Correspondents are more effective than grunts. Grunts merely kill the enemy. All that matters is what we write, what we photograph. History may be written with blood and iron but it's printed with ink. Grunts are good show business but we make them what they are. The lesser services like to joke about how every Marine platoon goes into battle accompanied by a platoon of Marine Corps photographers. That's affirmative. Marines fight harder because Marines have bigger legends to live up to."

Captain January slaps a large package on the floor by his desk. "And this is the final product of all our industry. My wife likes to show an interest in my work. She asked me for a souvenir. I'm sending her a gook."

Rafter Man's expression is so funny that I have to look away to avoid laughing out loud. "Sir?"

"Yes, Sergeant?"

"Where's the Top?"

"The First shirt went to Da Nang for some in-country R & R. You can see him after you come back from Hue." Captain January looks at his wristwatch. "Seventeen hundred. Chow time."

On the way to chow Rafter Man and I meet Chili Vendor and Daytona Dave and Mr. Payback at the ISO enlisted men's hootch. I give Rafter Man a utility jacket with 101st Airborne patches all over it. My own Army jacket has First Air Cavalry insignia. I select two salty sets of Army collar chevrons and we pin them on. Now we're Spec-5's—Army sergeants. Chili Vendor  and Daytona Dave and Mr. Payback are all buck sergeants from the Ninth Infantry Division.

We go to chow down in the Army mess hall. The Army eats real food. Cake, roast beef, ice cream, chocolate milk—all the bennies. Our own mess hall serves Kool-Aid and shit-on-a-shingle—chipped beef on toast—with peanut butter and jelly sandwiches for dessert.

"When's the Top due back?"

Chili Vendor says, "Oh, maybe tomorrow. January on your program again?"

I nod. "That fucking lifer. He's crazy. He's just plain fucking crazy. He gets crazier every time I see him. Now he's mailing a gook stiff home to his wife."

Daytona says, "There it is. But then the Top is a lifer, too."

"But the Top is decent. I mean, maybe the Crotch is his home, and he makes us do a good job, but he don't harass us with Mickey Mouse shit. He cuts the snuffies some slack when he can. The Top's not a lifer; he's a career Marine. Lifers are a breed. A lifer is anybody who abuses authority he doesn't deserve to have. There are plenty of civilian lifers."

The Army mess sergeant with the big cigar spot-checks I.D.'s.

The Army mess sergeant with the big cigar takes the shiny mess trays out of our hands and throws us out of his mess hall.

We retreat to the Marine mess hall where we eat shit-on-a-shingle and drink lukewarm Kool-Aid and we talk about how the Army could have at least sou-venired us some leftovers since that's all the Marine Corps ever gets anyway.

After chow we play tag back to our hootch. Laugh-ing and breathing hard, we take a moment to pull down the green plastic ponchos nailed on the outside of the hootch. During the night the ponchos will keep light in and rain out.

We lie on our racks and swap scuttlebutt. On the ceiling, the combat correspondent's motto in six-inch block letters: FIRST TO GO, LAST TO KNOW, WE WILL DEFEND TO THE DEATH OUR RIGHT TO BE MISINFORMED.

Mr. Payback performs his sea stories for Rafter Man: "The only difference between a sea story and a fairy tale is that a fairy tale begins with 'Once upon a time . . .' and a sea story begins with 'This is no shit'. Well, New Guy, listen up, because this is no shit. January orders me to play Monopoly. All fucking day. Every day of the fucking week. There's nothing lower than a lifer. They fuck me over, man, but I don't say a word. I do not say a word. Payback is a motherfucker, New Guy. Remember that. When Luke the gook zaps you in the back and Phantoms bury him in napalm canisters, that's payback. When you shit on people it comes back to you, sooner or later, only worse. My whole program is a mess because of lifers. But payback will come, sooner or later. I'd walk a mile for a payback."

I laugh. "Payback, you hate lifers because you *are* a lifer."

Mr. Payback lights up a joint. "You're the one who's tight with the lifers, Joker. Lifers take care of their own."

"Negative. The lifers are afraid to talk to me, I got so many ops."

"Operations? Shit." Mr. Payback turns to Rafter Man. "Joker thinks that the bad bush is down the road in the ville. He's never been in the shit. It's hard to talk about it. Like on Hastings—"

Chili Vendor interrupts: "You weren't on Operation Hastings, Payback. You weren't even in country."

64

"Oh, eat shit and die, you fucking Spanish American. You poge. I was *there*, man. I was in the shit with the grunts, man. Those guys have got guts, you know? They are very hard individuals. When you've been in the shit with grunts you're tight with them from then on, you know?"

I grunt. "Sea stories."

"Oh, yeah? How long you been in country, Joker? Huh? How much T.I. you got? How much fucking time in? Thirty months, poge. I got thirty months in country. I been there, man."

I say, "Don't listen to any of Mr. Payback's bullshit, Rafter Man. Sometimes he thinks he's John Wayne."

"That's affirmative," says Mr. Payback. "You listen to Joker, New Guy. He knows *ti ti*—very little. And if he ever does know anything it'll be because he learned it from me. You just know he's never been in the shit. He ain't got the stare."

Rafter Man looks up. "The what?"

"The thousand-yard stare. A Marine gets it after he's been in the shit for too long. It's like you've really seen . . . *beyond*. I got it. All field Marines got it. You'll have it, too."

Rafter Man says, "I will?"

Mr. Payback takes a few hits off the joint and then passes it to Chili Vendor. "I used to be an atheist, when I was a New Guy, a long time ago. . . ." Mr. Payback takes his Zippo lighter out of his shirt pocket and hands it to Rafter Man. "See? It says, 'You and me, God—right?'" Mr. Payback giggles. He seems to be trying to focus his vision on some distant object. "Yes, nobody is an atheist in a foxhole. You'll be praying."

Rafter Man looks at me, grins, hands the lighter

65

back to Mr. Payback. "There sure is a lot of stuff to learn."

I'm whittling a piece of ammo crate with my K-bar jungle knife. I'm carving myself a wooden bayonet.

Daytona Dave says, "Remember that gook kid that tried to eat the candy bar? It bit me. I was down in the ville, scarfing up some more orphans and that little Victor Charlie ambushed me. Ran up and bit the shit out of my hand." Daytona holds up his left hand, revealing a little red crescent of tooth marks. "The kid says that our chop-chop is number ten. I bet I get rabies."

Chili Vendor grins. He turns to Rafter Man. "There it is, New Guy. You'll know you're salty when you stop throwing C-ration cans *to* the kids and start throwing the cans *at* them."

I say, "I got to get back into the shit. I ain't heard a shot fired in anger in weeks. I'm bored to death. How are we ever going to get used to being back in the World? I mean, a day without blood is like a day without sunshine."

Chili Vendor say, "No sweat. The old *mamasan* that does our laundry tells us things even the lifers in Intelligence don't know. She says that in Hue the whole fucking North Vietnamese army is dug in deep inside an old fortress they call the Citadel. You won't come back, Joker. Victor Charlie is gonna shoot you in the heart. The Crotch will ship your scrawny little ass home in a three-hundred-dollar aluminum box all dressed up like a lifer in a blouse from a set of dress blues. But no white hat. And no pants. They don't give you any pants. Your friends from school and all of the relatives you never liked anyway will be at your funeral and they'll call you a good little

Christian and they'll say you were a hero to get wasted defeating Communism and you'll just lie there with a cold ass, dead as a mackerel."

Daytona Dave sits up. "You can be a hero for a little while, sometimes, if you can stop thinking about your own ass long enough, if you give a shit. But civilians don't know what to do, so they put up statues in the park for pigeons to drop turds on. Civilians don't know. Civilians don't want to know."

I say, "You guys are bitter. Don't you love the American way of life?"

Chili Vendor shakes his head. "No Victor Charlie ever raped my sister. Ho Chi Minh never bombed Pearl Harbor. We're prisoners here. We're prisoners of the war. They've taken away our freedom and they've given it to the gooks, but the gooks don't want it. They'd rather be alive than free."

I grunt. "There it is."


With my Magic Marker I "X" out a section of thigh on the nude woman outlined on the back of my flak jacket. The number 58 disappears. Fifty-seven days and a wake-up left in country.

Midnight. The boredom becomes unbearable. Chili Vendor suggests that we kill time by wasting our furry little friends.

I say, "Rat race!"

Chili Vendor hops off his canvas cot and into a corner. He breaks up a John Wayne cookie. In the corner, six inches off the deck, we've nailed a piece of ammo crate to form a triangular pocket. There's a little hole in the charred board. Chili Vendor puts the cookie fragments under the board. Then he snaps off the lights.

I toss Rafter Man one of my booties. Of course, he doesn't know what to do with it. "What—"

*Shhhh.*

We wait in ambush, enjoying the anticipation of violence. Five minutes. Ten minutes. Fifteen minutes. Then the Viet Cong rats crawl out of their holes. We freeze. The rats skitter along the rafters, climb down the screening, then hop onto the plywood deck, making little thumps, moving through the darkness without fear.

Chili Vendor waits until the skittering converges in the corner. Then he jumps out of his rack and flips on the overhead lights.

With the exception of Rafter Man we're all on our feet in the same second, forming a semicircle across the corner. The rats zip and zing, their tiny pink feet clawing for traction on the plywood. Two or three escape—so brave, or so terrified—in such situations motives are immaterial—that they run right over our feet and between our legs and through the deadly gauntlet of carefully aimed boots and stabbing bayonets.

But most of the rats herd together under the board.

Mr. Payback takes a can of lighter fluid from his bamboo footlocker. He squirts lighter fluid into the little hole in the board.

Daytona Dave strikes a match. "Fire in the hole!" He pitches the burning match into the corner.

The board *foomps* into flame.

Rats explode from beneath the board like shrapnel from a rodent grenade.

The rats are on fire. The rats are little flaming kamikaze animals zinging across the plywood deck, running under racks, over gear, around in circles, running faster and faster and in no particular direction except toward some place where there is no fire.

"GET SOME!" Mr. Payback is screaming like a lunatic. "GET SOME! GET SOME!" He chops a rat in half with his machete.

Chili Vendor holds a rat by the tail and, while it shrieks, pounds it to death with a boot.

I throw my K-bar at a rat on the other side of the hootch. The big knife misses the rat, sticks up in the floor.

Rafter Man doesn't know what to do.

Daytona Dave charges around and around with fixed bayonet, zeroing in on a burning rat like a fighter pilot in a dogfight. Daytona follows the rat's crazed, erratic course around and around, over all obstacles, gaining on him with every step. He buttstrokes the rat and then bayonets him, again and again and again. "That's one confirmed!"

And, as suddenly as it began, the battle is over.

After the rat race everyone collapses. Daytona is breathing hard and fast. "Whew. That was a good group. Real hard-core. I thought I was going to have a fucking heart attack."

Mr. Payback coughs, grunts. "Hey, New Guy, how many confirmed did you get?"

Rafter Man is still sitting on his canvas cot with my boot in his hand. "I . . . none. I mean, it happened so fast."

Mr. Payback laughs. "Well, sometimes it's fun to kill something you can see. You better get squared away, New Guy. Next time the rats will have guns."

Daytona Dave is wiping his face with a dirty green

skivvy shirt. "The New Guy will do okay. Cut him some slack. Rafter ain't got the killer instinct, that's all. Now me, I got about fifty confirmed. But everybody knows that gook rats drag off their dead."

We all throw things at Daytona Dave.

We rest for a while and then we gather up the barbecued rats and take them outside to hold a funeral in the dark.

Some guys from utilities platoon who live next door come out of their hootch to pay their respects.

Lance Corporal Winslow Slavin, honcho of the combat plumbers, struts up in a skuzzy green flight suit. The flight suit is ragged, covered with paint stains and oil splotches. "Only six? Shit. Last night my boys got seventeen. Confirmed."

I say, "Sounds like a squad of poges to me. Poges kill poges. These rats are Viet Cong field Marines. Hard-core grunts."

I pick up one of the rats. I turn to the combat plumbers. I hold up the rat and I kiss it.

Mr. Payback laughs, picks up one of the dead rats, bites off the tip of its tail. Then, swallowing, Mr. Payback says, "Ummm . . . love them crispy critters." He grins. He bends over, picks up another dead rat, offers it to Rafter Man.

Rafter Man is frozen. He can't speak. He just looks at the rat.

Mr. Payback laughs. "What's wrong, New Guy? Don't you want to be a killer?"

We bury the enemy rats with full military honors —we scoop out a shallow grave and we dump them in.

We sing:
>  *So come along and sing our song*
>  *And join our fam-i-ly ...*
>  *M.I.C. ... K.E.Y. ... M.O.U.S.E.*
>  *Mickey Mouse, Mickey Mouse. ...*

"Dear God," says Mr. Payback, looking up into the ugly sky. "These rats died like Marines. Cut them some slack. Ah-men."

We all say, "Ah-men."

After the funeral we insult the combat plumbers a few more times and then we return to our hootch. We lie awake in our racks. We discuss the battle and the funeral for a long time.

Then we try to sleep.

An hour later. It's raining. We roll up in our poncho liners and pray for morning. The monsoon rain is cold and heavy and comes without warning. Wind-blown water batters the ponchos hung around the hootch to protect us from the weather.

The terrible falling of the shells ...

*Incoming.*

"Oh, shit," somebody says. Nobody moves.

Rafter Man asks, "Is that—"

I say, "There it is."

The crumps start somewhere outside the wire and walk in like the footsteps of a monster. The crumps are becoming thuds. Thud. Thud. THUD. And then it's a whistle and a roar.

BANG.

The rain's rhythmic drumming is broken by the clang and rattle of shrapnel falling on our tin roof.

71

We're all out of our racks with our weapons in our hands like so many parts of the same body—even Rafter Man, who has begun to pick up on things.

Pounded by cold rain, we double-time to our bunker.

On the perimeter M-60 machine guns are banging and the M-79 grenade launchers are blooping and mortar shells are thumping out of the tubes.

Star flares burst all along the wire, beautiful clusters of green fire.

Inside our damp cave of sandbags we huddle elbow-to-elbow in wet skivvies, feeling the weight of the darkness, as helpless as cavemen hiding from a monster.

"I hope they're just fucking with us," I say. "I hope they're not going to hit the wire. I'm not ready for this shit."

Outside our bunker: BANG, BANG, BANG. And falling rain.

Each of us is waiting for the next shell to nail him right on the head—the mortar as an agent of existential doom.

A scream.

I wait for a time of silence and I crawl out to take a look. Somebody is down. The whistle of an incoming round forces me to retreat into the bunker. I wait for the shell to burst.

BANG.

I crawl out, stand up, and I run to the wounded man. He's one of the combat plumbers. "You utilities platoon? Where's Winslow?"

The man is whining. "I'm dying! I'm dying!" I shake him.

"Where's Winslow?"

"There." He points. "He was coming to help me. . . ."

Rafter Man and Chili Vendor come out and Rafter Man helps me carry the combat plumber to our bunker. Chili Vendor double-times off to get a corpsman.

We leave the combat plumber with Daytona and Mr. Payback and double-time through the rain, looking for Winslow.

He's in the mud outside his hootch, torn to pieces.

The mortar shells stop falling. The machine guns on the perimeter fade to short bursts. Even so, the grunts standing lines continue to pop green star clusters in case Victor Charlie plans to launch a ground attack.

Somebody throws a poncho over Winslow. The rain taps the green plastic sheet.

I say, "It took a lot of guts to do what Winslow did. I mean, you can see Winslow's guts and he sure had a lot of them."

Nobody says anything.

After the green ghouls from graves registration stuff Winslow into a body bag and take him away, we go back to our hootch. We flop on our racks, wasted.

I say, "Well, Rafter, now you've heard a shot fired in anger."

Soaking wet in green skivvies, Rafter Man is sitting on his rack. He has something in his hand. He's staring at it.

I sit up. "Hey, Rafter. What's that? You souvenir yourself a piece of shrapnel?" No response. "Rafter? You hit?"

Mr. Payback grunts. "What's wrong, New Guy? Did a few rounds make you nervous?"

Rafter Man looks up with a new face. His lips are twisted into a cold, sardonic smirk. His labored breathing is broken by grunts. He growls. His lips are wet with saliva. He's looking at Mr. Payback. The object in Rafter Man's hand is a piece of flesh, Winslow's flesh, ugly yellow, as big as a John Wayne cookie, wet with blood. We all look at it for a long time.

Rafter Man puts the piece of flesh into his mouth, onto his tongue, and we think he's going to vomit. Instead, he grits his teeth. Then, closing his eyes, he swallows.

I turn off the lights.

Dawn. The heat of the day comes quickly, burning away the mud puddles left by the monsoon rain. Rafter Man and I ditty-bop down to the Phu Bai landing zone. We wait for a med-evac chopper.

Ten minutes later a Jolly Green Giant comes in loaded.

Corpsmen run up the ramp at the rear of the vibrating machine and reappear immediately, carrying canvas stretchers. On the stretchers are bloody rags with men inside. Rafter Man and I run into the chopper. We lift a stretcher and run down the metal ramp. The chopper is already beginning to lift off.

We place the stretcher on the deck with the others, where the corpsmen are sorting the dead from the living, changing bandages, adjusting plasma bottles.

Rafter Man and I run into the prop wash, running sideways beneath the thumping blades into a tornado of hot wind and stinging gravel. We stop, hunched over, holding up our thumbs.

The chopper pilot is an invading Martian in an orange flame-retardant flight suit and an olive-drab space helmet. The pilot's face is a shadow behind a dark green visor. He gives us a thumbs-up. We run around to the cargo ramp and the door gunner gives us a hand up into the belly of the vibrating machine just as it lifts off.

The flight to Hue is north eight miles. Far below, Viet Nam is a patchwork quilt of greens and yellows. It's a beautiful country, especially when seen from the air. Viet Nam is like a page from a Marco Polo picture book. The deck is pockmarked with shell holes, and napalm air strikes have charred vast patches of earth, but the land is healing itself with beauty.

My ears pop. I pinch my nose and puff out my cheeks. Rafter Man imitates me. We sit on bales of green rubber-impregnated canvas body bags.

As we near Hue, the door gunner smokes marijuana and fires his M-60 machine gun at a farmer in the rice paddies below. The door gunner has long hair, a bushy moustache, and is naked except for an unbuttoned Hawaiian sport shirt. On the Hawaiian sport shirt are a hundred yellow hula dancers.

The hamlet beneath us is in a free fire zone—anybody can shoot at it at any time and for any reason. We watch the farmer run in the shallow water. The farmer knows only that his family needs some rice to eat. The farmer knows only that the bullets are tearing him apart.

He falls, and the door gunner giggles.

The med-evac chopper sets down on a landing zone near Highway One, a mile south of Hue. The LZ is cluttered with walking wounded, stretcher cases, and body bags. Before Rafter Man and I are off the LZ our chopper has been loaded with wounded and is airborne again, flying back to Phu Bai.

We wait for a rough rider convoy in front of a bombed-out gas station. Hours pass. Noon. I take off my flak jacket. I pull my old, ragged Boy Scout shirt out of my NVA rucksack. I put on the Boy Scout shirt so that the sun won't roast the flesh from my bones. On the frayed collar, corporal's chevrons that are so salty that the black enamel has worn off and the brass shows through. Over the right breast pocket, a cloth rectangle which reads *First Marine Division*, CORRE-SPONDENT. And in Vietnamese: BAO CHI.

Sitting on a bullet-riddled yellow oyster that says SHELL OIL, we drink Cokes that cost five dollars a bottle. The *mamasan* who sells us the Cokes is wearing a conical white hat. She bows every time we speak. She squawks and chatters like an old black bird. She flashes her black teeth at us. She is very proud of her teeth. Only a lifetime of chewing betel nuts can make teeth as black as hers. We don't understand a word of her magpie chatter, but the hatred in the smile frozen on her face says clearly, "Oh well, Americans may be assholes but they are very rich."

There is a popular sea story which says that old Victor Charlie *mamasans* sell Cokes with ground-up glass in them. Drinking, we wonder if that's true.

Two Dusters, light tanks with twin 40mm guns, grind by. The men in the Dusters ignore our thumbs.

An hour later a Mighty Mite zooms by at eighty miles an hour, the maximum speed of the little jeep. No luck.

Then a convoy of six-bys appears, led by two

M-48 Patton tanks. Thirty big trucks roar by at full speed. Two more Patton tanks are riding security at tail-end Charlie.

The first tank speeds up as it passes us.

The second tank slows down, bucks, jerks to a halt. In the turret is a blond tank commander who is not wearing a helmet or a shirt. He waves us on. We put on our flak jackets. We pick up our gear and swing it up onto the tank. Then Rafter Man and I climb up onto a block of hot, vibrating metal.

Down in a hatch by our feet is the driver. His head protrudes just enough for him to see; his hands are on the controls. The driver jerks the wobble stick and the tank lurches forward, bouncing, grinding, faster and faster and faster. The roar of an eight-hundred-horse-power diesel engine accelerates to a rhythmic rumble of mechanical power.

Rafter Man and I fall back against the hot turret. We are hanging onto the long ninety-millimeter gun like monkeys. The cool air of speed is delicious after hours in Viet Nam's one-hundred-and-twenty-degree yellow furnace. Our sweat-soaked shirts are cold. Flashing by: Vietnamese hootches, ponds with white ducks in them, circular graves with chipped and faded paint, and endless shimmering pieces of emerald water newly planted with rice.

It's a wonderful day. I'm so happy that I am alive, in one piece, and short. I'm in a world of shit, yes, but I am alive. And I am not afraid. Riding the tank gives me a thrilling sense of power and well-being. Who dares to shoot at the man who rides the tiger?

It's a beautiful tank. Painted on the long barrel: BLACK FLAG—*We Exterminate Household Pests*. Flying on a radio antenna, a ragged Confederate flag.

Military vehicles are beautiful because they are built from functional designs which make them real, solid, without artifice. The tank possesses the beauty of its hard lines; it is fifty tons of rolling armor on tracks like steel watchbands. The tank is our protection, rolling on and on forever, clanking out the dark mechanical poetry of iron and guns.

Suddenly the tank shifts to the left. Rafter Man and I are thrown hard into the turret. Metal grinds metal. The tank hits a bump, shifting sharply to the right and jerking to a halt, throwing us forward. Rafter man and I hang onto the gun and say, "Son-of-a-bitch . . ."

The blond tank commander climbs out of the turret hatch and jumps off the back of the tank.

The tank driver has run the tank off the road.

Fifty yards back a water buffalo is down on its back, legs out straight. The water bo bellows, tosses its curved horns. On the deck, in the center of the road, I see a tiny body, facedown.

Chattering Vietnamese civilians pour out of the roadside hootches, staring and pointing. The Vietnamese civilians crowd around to see how their American saviors have crushed the guts out of a child.

The blond tank commander speaks to the Vietnamese civilians in French. Then, walking back to the tank, the blond tank commander is pursued by an ancient *papasan*. There are tears in the *papasan's* eyes. The withered old man shakes his bony little fists and throws Asian curses at the tank commander's back. The Vietnamese civilians grow silent. Another child is dead, and, although it is very sad and painful, they accept it.

The blond tank commander climbs up onto his tank

and reinserts his legs into the turret hatch. "Iron Man, you fucking shitbird. You *will* drive this machine like it's a tank and not a goddamn sports car. You hit that little girl, you blind idiot. Hell, I could see her through the fucking vision blocks. She was standing on that water bo's back. . . ."

The driver turns, his face hard. "I didn't see them, skipper. What do they think they're doing, crossing in front of me like that? Don't these zipperheads know that tanks got the right-of-way?" The driver's face is coated with a thin film of oil and sweat; iron has entered into his soul and he has become a component of the tank, sweating oil to lubricate its meshing gears.

The blond tank commander says, "You fuck up one more time, Iron Man, and you *will* be a grunt."

The driver turns back to the front. "Aye-aye, sir. I'll watch the road, Lieutenant."

Rafter Man asks, "Sir, did we kill that girl? Why was that old man yelling at you?" Rafter Man looks sick.

The blond tank commander takes a green ballpoint pen and a little green notebook out of his hip pocket. He writes something in the notebook. "The little girl's grandfather? He was yelling about how he needs his water bo. He wants a condolence award. He wants us to pay him for the water bo."

Rafter Man doesn't say anything.

The blond tank commander yells at Iron Man: "Drive, you blind son-of-a-bitch."

And the tank rolls on.


On the outskirts of Hue, the ancient Imperial Capital, we see the first sign of the battle—a cathedral, centuries old, now a bullet-peppered box of ruined stone, roof caved in, walls punctured by shells.

Entering Hue, the third largest city in Viet Nam, is a strange new experience. Our war has been in the paddies, in hamlets where the largest structure was a bamboo hut. Seeing the effects of war upon a Vietnamese city makes me feel like a New Guy.

The weather is dreary but the city is beautiful. Hue has been beautiful for so long that not even war and bad weather can make it ugly.

Empty streets. Every building in Hue has been hit with some kind of ordnance. The ground is still wet from last night's rain. The air is cool. The whole city is enveloped in a white mist. The sun is going down.

We roll past a tank which has been gutted by B-40 rocket-propelled grenades. On the barrel of the shattered ninety-millimeter gun: BLACK FLAG.

Fifty yards down the road we pass two wasted sixbys. One of the big trucks has been knocked onto its side. The cab of the truck is a broken mass of jagged, twisted steel. The second six-by has burned and is only a skeleton of black iron. The windshields of both trucks have been strung with bright necklaces of bullet holes.

As we roll past Quoc Hoc High School I punch Rafter Man on the arm. "Ho Chi Minh went there," I say. "I wonder if Uncle Ho played varsity basketball. I wonder who Uncle Ho took to the senior prom."

Rafter Man grins.

Shots pop, far away. Single rounds. Short bursts of automatic weapons. The fighting has stopped, for the moment. The shots we hear are just some grunt trying to get lucky.

Near the University of Hue the tank grinds to a halt and Rafter Man and I hop off. The University of Hue is now a collection point for refugees on their way to Phu Bai. Whole families with all of their possessions have occupied the classrooms and corridors since the battle began. The refugees are too tired to run anymore. The refugees look cold and drained the way you look after death sits on your face and smothers you for so long that you get tired of screaming. Outside, the women cook pots of rice. All over the deck there are piles of human shit.

We wave good-bye to the blond tank commander and his tank grumbles and rolls away. The tank's steel cleats crush some bricks which have been thrown into the street by explosions.

Rafter Man and I stare across the River of Perfumes. We stare at the Citadel. The river is ugly. The river is muddy. The steel suspension bridge—The Bridge of the Golden Waters—is down, blown by enemy frogmen. Torn girders jut out of the dark water like the broken bones of a sea serpent.

A hand grenade explodes, far away, inside the Citadel.

Rafter Man and I head for the MAC-V, Military Assistance Command—Viet Nam, compound.

"This is a beautiful place," says Rafter Man.

"It was. It really was. I've been here a few times for award ceremonies. General Cushman was here. I took his picture and he took a picture of me taking a picture of him. And Ky was here, all duded up in his black silk flight jacket with silver general's stars all over it and a black cap with silver general's stars all over that, too. Ky had these pearl-handled pistols and wore a purple ascot. He looked like a Japanese playboy. He had his program squared away, that Ky. He believed in a Viet Nam for the Vietnamese. I guess

81

that's why we kicked him out. But he was beautiful that day. You should have seen all the schoolgirls in their *ao dai*, purple and white, carrying their little parasols. . . ."

"Where are they now? The girls?"

"Oh, dead, I guess. Did you know that there's a legend that Hue rose from a pool of mud as a lotus flower?"

"Look at that!"

A squad of Arvins are looting a mansion. The Arvins of the Army of the Republic of Viet Nam look funny because all of their equipment is too big for them. In baggy uniforms and oversized helmets they look like little boys playing war.

I say, "Decent. Number one. We got some slack, Rafter. Remember this, Rafter Man, any time you can see an Arvin you are safe from Victor Charlie. The Arvins run like rabbits at the first sign of violence. An Arvin infantry platoon is about as lethal as a garden club of old ladies throwing marshmallows. Don't believe all that scuttlebutt about Arvins being cowards. They just hate the Green Machine more than we do. They were drafted by the Saigon government, which was drafted by the lifers who drafted us, who were drafted by the lifers who think that they can buy the war. And Arvins are not stupid. The Arvins are not stupid when they are doing something they enjoy, like stealing. Arvins sincerely believe that jewels and money are essential military supplies. So we're safe until the Arvins start yelling, 'Beaucoup VC, beaucoup VC!' and then run away. But be careful. Arvins are always shooting at chickens, other people's pigs, and trees. Arvins will shoot anything except transistor

radios, Coca-Colas, sunglasses, money, and the enemy."

"Don't they get money from their government?"

I grin. "Money *is* their government."

The sun is gone. Rafter Man and I double-time. A
sentry challenges us; I tell him to go to hell.

Fifty-six days and a wake-up.

In the morning we wake up inside the MAC-V compound, a white two-story building with bullet-pocked
walls. The compound has been enclosed behind a wall
of sandbags and concertina wire.

We gather up our gear and prepare to leave while a
light colonel reads a statement made by the military
mayor of Hue. The statement is a denial that there is
looting in Hue and a warning that looters will be shot
on sight. A dozen civilian war correspondents sit on
the deck, wiping sleep from their eyes, half-listen-
ing, yawning. Then the light colonel adds a personal
comment. Someone has awarded a Purple Heart to a
big white goose that got wounded while the compound was under attack. The light Colonel feels that
the civilian correspondents do not understand that
war is serious business.

Outside, I point to a wasted NVA hanging in the
wire. "War is serious business, son, and this is our
gross national product." I kick the corpse, triggering
panic in the maggots in the hollow eye sockets and
in the grinning mouth and in each of the bullet holes
in his chest. "Gross?"

Rafter Man kneels down to get a better look. "Yes,
he is confirmed."

A CBS camera crew appears, surrounded by starstruck grunts who strike combat-Marine poses, pretending to be what they are. They all want Walter Cronkite to meet their sisters. In white short-sleeved shirts the CBS cameramen hurry off to photograph death in living color.

I stop a master sergeant. "Top, we want to get into the shit."

The master sergeant is writing on a piece of yellow paper on a clipboard. He doesn't look up, but jerks his thumb over his shoulder. "Across the river. One-Five. Get a boat ride by the bridge."

"One-Five? Outstanding. Thanks, Top."

The master sergeant walks away, writing on the yellow paper. He ignores four skuzzy grunts who run into the compound, each man holding up one corner of a poncho. On the poncho is a dead Marine. The grunts are screaming for a corpsman and when they put the poncho down, very gently, a pool of dark blood pours out onto the concrete deck.

Rafter Man and I hurry down to the River of Perfumes. We talk to a baby-faced Navy ensign who souvenirs us a ride on a Vietnamese gunboat ferrying reinforcements to the Vietnamese Marines.

As we skim down the river Rafter Man asks, "Are these guys any good?"

I nod. "The best the Arvins got. They're not as tough as the Korean Marines, though. The ROK's are so hard that they got muscles in their shit. The Blue Dragon Brigade. I was on an op with them down by Hoi An."

A shot pops from the shore. The bullet buzzes over.

The gunboat crew opens up with a fifty-caliber machine gun and a forty mike-mike cannon.

Rafter Man watches with joy in his eyes as the bullets knock up thin stalks of water along the river bank. He holds his piece at port arms, first to fight.

The Strawberry Patch, a large triangle of land between the Citadel and the River of Perfumes, is a quiet suburb of Hue. We get off the gunboat at the Strawberry Patch and wander around with the Vietnamese Marines until we see a little Marine with an expensive pump shotgun slung across his back, a case of C rations on his shoulder, and DEADLY DELTA on his flak jacket.

I say, "Hey, bro, where's One-Five?"

The little Marine turns, smiles.

I say, "You need a huss with that?"

"No thanks, Marine. You people One-One?"

"No, sir," I say. Officers do not wear rank insignia in the field but snuffies learn to fix a man's rank by his voice. "We're looking for One-Five. I got a bro in the First Platoon. They call him Cowboy. He wears a cowboy hat."

"I'm Cowboy's platoon commander. The Lusthog Squad is in the platoon area up by the Citadel."

We walk along with the little Marine.

"I'm Joker, sir. Corporal Joker. This is Rafter Man. We work for *Stars and Stripes*."

"My name is Bayer. Robert M. Bayer the third. My people call me Shortround, for obvious reasons. You here to make Cowboy famous?"

I laugh. "Never happen."

The gray sky is clearing. The white mist is moving away, exposing Hue to the sun.

First Platoon's area is within sight of the massive walls of the Citadel. While First Platoon waits for the attack to begin, the Lusthog Squad is partying.

Crazy Earl points a forefinger at the three of us. "Resupply! Number one!" Then: "Hey, cowpuncher, the Joker is on deck."

Cowboy looks up and grins. He's holding a large brown bottle of tiger piss—Vietnamese beer. "Well, *no* shit. It's the Joker and his New Guy. *Lai dai*, bros, come on, sit and share, sit and share."

Rafter Man and I sit down in the dirt and Cowboy throws loose stacks of Vietnamese piasters into our laps. I laugh, surprised. I pick up the brightly colored bills, large bills, in large denominations. Cowboy shoves bottles of tiger piss into our hands.

"Hey, Skipper!" says Cowboy. "Souvenir me spaghetti and meatballs, okay? Every time we chow down I pull ham and mothers—the Breakfast of Champions. I hate fucking ham and lima beans."

The little Marine rips open one case of C's, pulls out a cardboard box, pitches it to Cowboy.

Cowboy catches the box, squints at the label. "Number one. Thanks, Skipper."

Crazy Earl throws another stack of piasters into my lap.

Every man in the squad has a pile of money.

"Man, we finally got paid," says Crazy Earl. "You know what I am saying, gentlemen? We been slave-labor mercenaries and now we are rich. We got a million P's here, gentlemen. Yes, that's beaucoup P's."

I say, "Sir, where'd this money—"

Mr. Shortround shrugs. "Money? I don't see any money." He takes off his helmet. On the back of the helmet: *Kill a Commie for Christ*. Mr. Shortround

86

lights a cigarette. "About half a million P's. Maybe a thousand dollars per man in American money."

Cowboy says, "You got to write about our John Wayne lieutenant." Cowboy punches Mr. Shortround on the arm. "Mr. Shortround is a mustang. When the Crotch made him a lieutenant he was just a corporal, just a snuffy like us. He's very little, but he is oh so bad." Cowboy tilts his head back and sucks in a long swallow of tiger piss. Then: "We were taking this railroad terminal. That's where the safe was. We blew it open with a block of C-4. The gooks were coming down on us with automatic weapons, B-40's, even a fucking mortar. The Lieutenant got six confirmed. Six! He wasted those zipperheads like a born killer."

"There are NVA here," says Crazy Earl. "Many, many of them."

"That's affirmative," says Cowboy. "And they are as hard as slant-eyed drill instructors. They are highly motivated individuals."

Crazy Earl holds his bottle by the neck and smashes it across a fallen statue of a fat, smiling, bald-headed gook. "This ain't a war, it's a series of overlapping riots. We blow them away. They come up behind us before we're out of sight and shoot us in the ass. I know a guy in One-One that shot a gook and then tied a satchel charge to him and blew him into little invisible pieces because shooting gooks is a waste of time—they come back to life. But these gooks piss you off so bad that you got to shoot *some*thing, *any*thing. Bros, half the confirmed kills I got are civilians and the other half is water buffaloes." Earl pauses, burps, drawing the burp out as long as he can. "You should have seen Animal Mother wasting those Arvins. As soon as we hit the shit the Arvins started *di-di mau-*

ing for the rear and Animal Mother spit and then blew them away."

"I miss Stumbling Stewey," says Alice, the black giant. He explains to me and Rafter Man: "Stumbling Stewey was our honcho before Stoke, the Supergrunt. Stumbling Stewey was real nervous, you know? Very nervous. I mean, he was *nervous*. The only way the dude could relax was throwing hand grenades. He was always popping frags all over the area. Then he started holding on to them right up to the last second. So one day ol' Stumbling Stewey pulled the pin and just stood there, staring, just staring and staring at that little ol' olive-drab egg in his hand. . . ."

Crazy Earl nods, burps. "I was just a New Guy the day Stumbling Stewey blew himself away and Stoke the Supergrunt took the squad. Stoke made me assistant squad leader. He could see that I didn't know nothing, and all that good shit, but he said he liked my personality." Crazy Earl takes a swallow from another bottle of beer. "Hey, Cowboy, get your horse! Quick! My crabs are having a rodeo!"

Donlon, the radioman, says, "I hope we stay here. This street fighting is decent duty. We can see them here. We got cover, resupply, even some areas where you can cut a few Z's without digging a hole. No rice paddies full of slope shit to swim in. No immersion foot. No jungle rot. No leeches falling from the trees."

Crazy Earl flips a beer bottle into the air and the bottle arches down and smashes upon a broken wall. "Affirmative, but we blow up all these shrines and temples and then the gooks got lots of shit to hide under and we have to dig them out."

Everybody gets a little high. Crazy Earl goes into a long, detailed sea story about how the Montagnard

Tribesmen are in fact Viet Cong cavemen. "We said we were going to bomb them back to the Stone Age and we do not lie."

Cowboy suggests that Montagnards are actually Viet Cong Indians and that the secret to winning the war is to issue each grunt a horse. Then Victor Charlie would have to hump while Marines could ride.

Crazy Earl puts his arm across the shoulders of the man next to him. The man has a bush cover pulled down over his face, a beer in his hand, a pile of money in his lap. "This is my bro," says Crazy Earl, removing the bush cover from the man's face. "This is his party. He is the guest of honor. You see, today is his birthday."

Rafter Man looks at me, his mouth open. "Sarge . . ."

I say, "Don't call me Sarge."

The man next to Crazy Earl is a dead man, a North Vietnamese corporal, a clean-cut Asian kid about seventeen years old with ink-black hair, cropped short.

Crazy Earl hugs the North Vietnamese corporal. He grins. "I made him sleep." Crazy Earl puts his forefinger to his lips and whispers, "Shhh. He's resting now."

Before Rafter Man can start asking questions Animal Mother and another Marine double-time up the road, carrying a large cardboard box between them. They drop the box and reach inside. They throw plastic bags to each of us. "Resupply! Resupply! Get your red-hot bennies. Scarf it up!"

Cowboy snatches up his bag and rips it open. "Long-rats. Outstanding!"

I pick up my bag and I show it to Rafter Man.

"This is number one chow, Rafter. The Army eats this shit on humps. Add water and you got real food."

Lieutenant Shortround says, "Okay, Mother, where'd you souvenir the chow?"

Animal Mother spits. He grins, baring rotten teeth. "I stole it."

"You stole it, sir."

"Yeah, I stole it . . . *sir.*"

"That's looting. They shoot people for that."

"I stole it from the Army . . . *sir.*"

"Outstanding. It is part of your duty as a Marine to harass our sister services. Carry on."

Cowboy punches the Marine who helped Animal Mother carry the cardboard box. "This is T.H.E. Rock. Make him famous. He wears that rock around his neck so that when the dinks zap him they'll know who he is."

T.H.E. Rock grins. "You fucking alcoholic. I wish you'd stop telling people about my rock." He pulls out a rawhide cord and shows us his rock, a quartz crystal mounted in brass.

Animal Mother props his M-60 machine gun against a wall and sits down, cross-legged. "Man, I almost got me some eatin' pussy."

T.H.E. Rock says, "That's affirmative. Mother was chasing a little gook girl with his dick hanging out. . . ."

Lieutenant Shortround pulls his K-bar from its sheath and cuts a chunk from a block of C-4 plastic explosive he has extracted from a Claymore mine. He puts the piece of C-4 into a little stove he has made by punching air holes into an empty C rations can. He strikes a match and lights the C-4. He fills a second can with water from his canteen and then holds the can of water over the blue flame. "Mother, you *know* what I told you last week."

A Phantom F-4 jet roars over and unloads a few rocket pods into the Citadel. Explosions rock the deck.

T.H.E. Rock looks at Animal Mother as he explains: "She was just a baby, sir. Thirteen or fourteen."

Animal Mother grins, spits. "If she's old enough to bleed she's old enough to butcher."

Mr. Shortround looks at Animal Mother, but doesn't say anything. He takes a white plastic spoon out of his shirt pocket and puts it into the can of boiling water. Then he takes a tinfoil packet of cocoa out of his thigh pocket, tears it open, pours the brown powder into the can of boiling water. He takes hold of the white plastic spoon and begins to stir the hot chocolate slowly. "Animal Mother? Do you hear me? I'm talking to you."

Animal Mother glares at the lieutenant. Then, "Oh, I was just fooling around, Lieutenant."

Mr. Shortround stirs his hot chocolate.

I say, "Animal Mother, how come you think you're so bad?"

Animal Mother looks at me, surprised. "Hey, motherfucker, don't even talk to me. You ain't a grunt. You want your face stomped in? Huh? You want to battle?"

I pick up my M-16.

Animal Mother reaches for his M-60.

Cowboy says, "Man, if there's one thing I can't stand, it's violence. I mean, if you got to blow Mother away, that's outstanding. Nobody likes Mother anyway. Shit, he don't even like himself. But you got to get a real gun, not that toy M-16. If it's Mattel, it's swell." Cowboy unhooks a frag from his flak jacket and tosses it to me. "Here. Use this."

I catch the hand grenade. I toss it up into the air a few times, catching it, still looking at Animal Mother. "No, I'm going to get me an M-60 and then me and this motherfucker are going to have one duel—"

"Stow it, Joker," Mr. Shortround interrupts: "Animal Mother, listen up. You harass one more little girl and I'm going to put my little silver bar in my pocket and then you and I are going to throw some hands."

Animal Mother grunts, spits, picks up a bottle of tiger piss. He hooks a tooth into the metal cap and forces the bottle up. The cap pops off. He takes a swallow, then looks at me. He mutters, "Fucking poge . . ." He takes another couple of swallows and then says very loud, "Cowboy, you remember when we was set up in that L-shaped ambush up by Khe Sanh and blew away that NVA rifle squad? You remember that little gook bitch that was guiding them? She was a lot younger than the one I saw today." He takes another swallow. "I didn't get to fuck that one either. But that's okay. That's okay. I shot her motherfucking face off." Animal Mother burps. He looks at me and smirks. "That's affirmative, poge. I shot her motherfucking face off."

Alice shows me a necklace of little bones and tries to convince me that they're magic Voodoo bones from New Orleans, but they look like dry old chicken bones to me.

"We . . . are animals," I say.

After a couple of minutes Crazy Earl says, "Grunts ain't animals. We just do our job. We're shot at and missed, shit on and hit. The gooks are grunts, like us. They fight, like us. They got lifer poges running their country and we got lifer poges running ours. But at least the gooks are grunts, like us. Not the Viet Cong. The VC are some dried-up old *mamasans* with rusty carbines. The NVA, man, we are tight with the NVA. We kill each other, no doubt about it, but we're tight. We're hard." Crazy Earl tosses an empty beer bottle to the deck and picks up his Red Ryder air rifle. He fires the air rifle at the bottle and the BB ricochets off the bottle with a faint *ping*. "I love the little commie bastards, man. I really do. Grunts understand grunts. These are great days we are living, bros. We are jolly green giants, walking the earth with guns. The people we wasted here today are the finest individuals we will ever know. When we rotate back to the World we're gonna miss having somebody around who's worth shooting. There ought to be a government for grunts. Grunts could fix the world up. I never met a grunt I didn't like, except Mother."

I say, "Never happen. It would make too much sense. It's better that we save Viet Nam from the people who live here. Of course, they love us; we'll kill them if they don't. When you've got them by the balls their hearts and minds will follow."

Donlon says, "Well, we're rich and we got beaucoup beer and beaucoup chow. Now all we need is the Bob Hope show."

I stand up. The beer has gone to my head. "I'll be Bob Hope." I hesitate. I touch my face. "Oh, wow, my nose ain't big enough." Mild laughter.

A hundred yards away a heavy machine gun fires a long burst. Scattered small arms fire replies.

I do impressions.

"Friends, I am Bob Hope. You all remember me, I'm sure. I was in some movies with Bing Crosby. Well, I'm here in Viet Nam to entertain you. The folks back home don't care enough about you to bring you back to the World so you won't get wasted, but they do care enough to send comedians over here so that at least you can die laughing. So have you heard the one about the Viet Nam veteran who came home and said, 'Look, Mom, no hands!' "

The squad laughs. They say: "Do John Wayne!"

Doing my John Wayne voice, I tell the squad a joke: "Stop me if you've heard this. There was a Marine of nuts and bolts, half robot—weird but true— whose every move was cut from pain as though from stone. His stoney little hide had been crushed and broken. But he just laughed and said, 'I've been crushed and broken before.' And, sure enough, he had the heart of a bear. His heart functioned for weeks after it had been diagnosed by doctors. His heart weighed half a pound. His heart pumped seven hundred thousand gallons of warm blood through one hundred thousand miles of veins, working hard—hard enough in twelve hours to lift one sixty-five-ton boxcar one foot off the deck. He said. The world would not waste the heart of a bear, he said. On his clean blue pajamas many medals hung. He was a walking word of history, in the shop for a few repairs. He took it on the chin and was good. One night in Japan his life came out of his body—black—like a question mark. If you can keep your head while others are losing theirs perhaps you have misjudged the situation. Stop me if you've heard this. . . ."

Nobody says anything.

"The war is ruining my sense of humor," I say. I squat.

Cowboy nods. "There it is. All I'm doing is counting my days, just counting my days. A hundred days and a wake-up and I'll be on that big silver Freedom Bird, flying back to the World, back to the block, back to the Lone Star State, back to the land of the big PX. And I'll have medals all over myself. And I won't be fucked up. No, when you get fucked up they send you to Japan. You go to Japan and somebody pins a medical discharge to what's left of you and all that good shit."

"I'd rather be wasted," I say. "Hire the handicapped—they're fun to watch."

Cowboy grins.

T.H.E. Rock says, "You know, my mom writes me a lot of letters about what a brave boy the Rock is. The Rock is not a boy; he's a person." He drinks beer. "I know I'm a person because I know there ain't no Santa Claus. There ain't no fucking Easter bunny. You know? Back in the World we thought that the future is always safe in a little gold box somewhere. Well, I'll live forever. I'm the Rock."

Crazy Earl grunts. "Hey Skipper, what say we stuff some dope into your shotgun and toke it through the barrel?"

Mr. Shortround shakes his head. "No can do, Craze. We're moving most skosh."

Donlon is talking into his handset. "Sir, the C.O. wants the Actual."

Donlon gives the handset to Mr. Shortround. The Lieutenant talks to Delta Six, the commanding officer of Delta One-Five.

"Number ten. Just when we were scarfing up some

of the bennies," says Crazy Earl. "Just when we were getting a little piece of slack. . . ."

Lieutenant Shortround stands up and starts putting on his gear. "Moving, rich kids. Saddle up. Craze, get your people on their feet."

"Moving. Moving."

We all stand up, except for the NVA corporal who remains seated, a beer in his hand, a pile of money in his lap, his split lips curled back in a death grin.

Alice steps up with a machete in one hand and a blue canvas shopping bag in the other. He kneels. With two blows of the machete Alice chops off the NVA corporal's feet. He picks up each foot by the big toe and drops it into the blue shopping bag. "This gook was a very hard dude. Number one! Big Magic!"

The grunts stuff beer bottles, piasters, long-rats, and looted souvenirs into their baggy pockets, into Marine-issue field packs, and into NVA haversacks souvenired from enemy grunts they have wasted. The grunts pick up their weapons.

Moving. Moving. I walk behind Cowboy. Rafter Man walks behind me.

I say, "Well, I guess this Citadel shit is going to be oh so bad. But it could be worse. I mean, at least it's not Parris Island."

Cowboy grins. He says, "There it is."


We see the great walls of the Citadel. With zigzagging ramparts thirty feet high and eight feet thick, surrounded by a moat, the fortress looks like an ancient castle from a fairy tale about dragons who guard treasure and knights on white horses and princesses in need of assistance. The castle is black stone against a cold gray sky, with dark towers populated by shadows that are alive.

The Citadel is actually a small walled city constructed by French engineers as protection for the home of Gia Long, Emperor of the Annamese Empire. When Hue was the Imperial Capital, the Citadel protected the Emperor and the royal family and the ancient treasure of the Forbidden City from pirates raiding from the South China Sea.

We are big white American boys in steel helmets and heavy flak jackets, armed with magic weapons, laying siege to a castle in modern times. One-Five has changed a lot since the days when it was the first battalion to hit the beach at Guadacanal.

Metal birds flash in and shit steel eggs all over the place. F-4 Phantom jet fighters are dropping napalm, high explosives, and Willy Peter—white phosphorus. With bombs we are expressing ourselves; we are writing our history in shattered blocks of stone.

Black roses of smoke bloom inside the Citadel.

We ditty-bop Indian-file along both sides of the road, twenty yards between each man. The lines pop and snick as cocking levers are snapped back and bolts sent home, chambering rounds. Safeties are clicked off. Selector switches are thumbed to the full automatic position. Those Marines armed with M-14's fix bayonets.

Machine guns start typing out history. First our guns, then theirs. Snipers on the wall fire a round here and there, sighting us in.

War is a catalogue of sounds. Our ears direct our feet.

A bullet crunches into a wall.

Somebody starts singing:

*M.I.C. . . . K.E.Y. . . . M.O.U.S.E.*

The machine guns are exchanging a steady fire now, like old friends having a conversation. Thumps and thuds puncture the rhythm of the bullets.

The snipers zero in on us. Each shot becomes a word spoken by death. Death is talking to us. Death wants to tell us a funny secret. We may not like death but death likes us. Victor Charlie is hard but he never lies. Guns tell the truth. Guns never say, "I'm only kidding." War is ugly because the truth can be ugly and war is very sincere.

I say out loud: "You and me, God—right?"

I send guard-mail directives to my personal Tactical Area of Responsibility, which extends to the perimeters of my skin. Dear Feet, tiptoe through the tulips. Balls, hang in there. Legs, don't do any John Waynes. My body is serviceable. I intend to maintain my body in the excellent condition in which it was issued.

In the silence of our hearts we speak to our werewolf weapons; our weapons reply.

Cowboy is listening to me mutter to myself. "John Wayne? Hey, Joker's right. This ain't real. This is just a John Wayne movie. Joker can be Paul Newman. I'll be a horse."

"Yeah."

Crazy Earl says, "Can I be Gabby Hayes?"

"The Rock can be a rock," says Donlon, the radioman.

Alice says, "I'll be Ann-Margret."

"Animal Mother can be a rabid buffalo," says Stutten, honcho of the third fire team.

The walls are assaulted by werewolf laughter.

"Who'll be the Indians?"

The little enemy folks audition for the part—machine-gun bullets rip across a wall to starboard.

Lieutenant Shortround calls up his squad leaders with a hand signal—he holds up his right hand and twirls it. Three squad leaders, including Crazy Earl, double-time to him. He talks to them, points at the wall. The squad leaders double-time back to their squads to confer with their fire team leaders.

Lieutenant Shortround blows a whistle and then we're all running like big-assed birds. We don't want to do this. We are all afraid. But if you stayed behind you would be alone. Your friends are going; you go too. You're not a person anymore. You don't have to be who you are anymore. You're part of an attack, one green object in a line of green objects, running toward a breach in the Citadel wall, running through hard noise and bursting metal, running, running, running . . . you don't look back.

We double-time, werewolves with guns, panting. We run as though impatient to sink into the darkness that is opening up to swallow us. Something snaps and we're past the point of no return. We're going through the broken wall. We're running fast and we aren't going to stop. Nothing can stop us.

The air is being torn.

The deck shifts beneath your feet. The asphalt sucks at your feet like sand on the beach.

Green tracer bullets dissect the sky.

Bullets hit the street. The impact of the bullets is the sound of a covey of quail taking flight. And sparks. You feel the shock of bullets punching through bricks. Splinters of stone sting your face.

People tell you what to do.

Keep moving, keep moving, keep moving. If you stop moving, if you hesitate, your heart will stop beating. Your legs are machines winding you up like a mechanical toy. If your legs stop moving, your taut spring will run down and you will fall over, a lump without motion.

You feel like you could run around the world. Now the asphalt is a trampoline and you are fast and graceful, a green jungle cat.

Sounds. Cardboard being torn. Head-on collisions. Trains derailing. Walls falling into the sea.

Metal hornets swarm overhead.

Pictures: The dark eyes of guns; the cold eyes of guns. Pictures blink and blur, a wall, tiny men, shattered blocks of stone.

Keep moving, keep moving, keep moving. . . .

Your feet take you up . . . up . . . over the rubble of the wall . . . up . . . up . . . you're loving it . . . climbing, you're not human, you're an animal, you feel like a god . . . you scream: "DIE! DIE! DIE, YOU MOTHERFUCKERS! DIE! DIE! DIE!"

Hornets try to swarm into you—you swat them aside.

Boots crunch in powdered stone. Equipment flaps, clangs, and rattles. People curse.

"Oh, *fuck*."

Keep moving.

Your Boy Scout shirt is wet with sweat. Salty sweat wiggles into your eyes and onto your lips. Your right index finger is on the trigger of your M-16. Here I come, you say to yourself, here I come with a gun full of bullets. How many rounds left in this magazine? How many days left to my rotation date? Am I carrying too much gear? Where *are* they? And where the hell are my feet?

A face. The face moves. Your weapon sights in. Your M-16 automatic rifle vibrates. The face is gone.

Keep moving.

And then your feet no longer touch the ground and you wonder what's happening to you. Your body relaxes, then goes rigid. You hear the sound of a human body erupting, the ugly sound of a human body being torn apart by high-speed metal. The pictures blinking before your eyes slow down like a silent film on a defective reel. Your weapon floats out of your hands and suddenly you are alone. You are floating. Up. Up. You are being lifted up by a wall of sound. The pictures blink faster and faster and suddenly the filmstrip snaps and the wall of sound slams into you —total, terrible sound. The deck is enormous as you fall. You merge with the earth. Your flak jacket absorbs much of the impact. Your helmet falls off your head and spins. You're on your back, crushed by sound. You think: Is that the sky?

"CORPSMAN," someone says, far away. "CORPSMAN!"

You're on your back. All around you boots dance by, pounding and crunching. Dirt clods and pieces of stone fall from the sky, into your mouth, your eyes. You spit out stone. You hold up one of your hands. You try to tell the pounding boots: Hey, don't step on me.

Your palms are hot. Your legs are broken. With one of your hands you touch yourself, your face, your thighs, you search your broken guts for warm, wet cavities.

Your reaction to your own death is nothing more than a highly intensified curiosity.

A hand presses you down. You wonder if you should try to do something about your broken legs. You think that it's possible that you don't have any legs. Tons of ocean water, dark and cold and populated by monsters, are crushing you. You try to raise your head. Hands hold you down. You fight. You fling your arms. Strong hands search for damage in your body.

"Legs . . ."

You cough up spiders.

On the ground beside you is a Marine without a head. Exhibit A, formerly a person, now two hundred pounds of fractured meat. The Marine without a head is on his back. His face has been knocked off. The top of his skull has been torn back, with the soft brain inside. The jawbone and bottom teeth are intact. In the hands of the Marine without a head is an M-60 machine gun, locked there forever by rigor mortis. His finger is on the trigger. His canvas jungle boots are muddy.

You look at the dried mud on the jungle boots of the Marine without a head and you are stunned that his feet look so much like your own.

You reach out. You touch his hand.

Something stings your arm.

Suddenly, you are very tired. You are breathing hard from the running. Your heart is beating so hard that it seems to want to tear its way out of your body. Through the center of your heart there is a star-shaped bullet hole.

Hands touch you. Gentle hands. "You're okay, jarhead. No sweat. I'm Doc Jay. Can you hear me? You can trust me, Marine. I got magic hands."

"No," you say. "NO!" You try to explain to the hands that part of you is missing in action. You want the hands to find the missing part; you don't want your missing part to be left behind. But you cannot speak. Your mouth won't work.

You sleep. You trust the hands that are holding you, the hands that are lifting you up.

In your dope dream of death you are an enlistment poster nailed to a black wall: THE MARINE CORPS BUILDS MEN—BODY—MIND—SPIRIT.

You feel yourself breaking up into three pieces . . . you hear strange voices . . .

"What's *wrong*?" one voice says, confused and frightened. "What's *wrong*?"

"Who's there?"

"What?"

"Who's there?"

"I'm Mind. Are you—"

"Affirmative. I'm his Body. I'm not feeling well. . . ."

"This is utterly ridiculous," interjects a third voice. "This can't be happening."

"Who said that?" Mind demands. "Body? That you?"

"I said it, fool. You may call me Spirit."

Body sneers. "I don't believe either of you."

Mind speaks slowly: "Now, we've got to be logical about this. Our man is down. We've got to get organized."

Body whimpers. "Listen, you guys, that's *me* lying

there—not you. You don't know what it's like."

Mind says, "Look, you moron, we're all in this together. If he goes, we all go."

"Is he . . ." Body can't say the word. "I've *got* to survive."

"No," Mind observes. "Not necessarily. They play this game. I'm not sure we are allowed to interfere."

Body is horrified. "What kind of 'game'?"

"I'm not sure. Something about rules. They have a lot of rules."

Spirit says, "This guy pisses me off. I'm not going back."

Mind says, "You *have* to go back."

"On the contrary," says Spirit. "I do as I please. You two have no control over me."

"Forget him," says Body.

Mind insists, "But Spirit *must* return with us."

"*No.* We don't need him."

Mind considers the situation. "Perhaps Spirit has a valid argument. Perhaps I shouldn't go back either. . . ."

Body is frantic. "NO! PLEASE. . . ."

"Yet, actually, nothing would be achieved by not going back. Our actions will not affect their game in any event. Losing one man won't change the game one way or the other. In fact, losing men seems to be the whole point of the game. We must be practical. Come along, Body, we're going back."

Spirit says, "Tell the man I'm missing in action."

In your dream you call for Chaplain Charlie. You met the Navy chaplain when you interviewed him for a feature article you were writing. Chaplain Charlie was an amateur magician. With his magic, Chaplain Charlie entertained Marines in sick bays and distributed spiritual tourniquets to men who were still alive, but weaponless. To brutal, godless children Chaplain Charlie spoke about how God is merciful, despite appearances, about how the Ten Commandments lack detail because when you're writing on stone tablets with lightening bolts you've got to be brief, about how the Free World will conquer Communism with the aid of God and a few Marines, and about free fish. One day a Vietnamese child boobytrapped Chaplain Charlie's black bag of tricks. Chaplain Charlie reached in and pulled out a bright ball of death. . . .

"Hey, hit the deck, leatherneck, we're moving."

"What—?" I recognize the rooms I'm in. I remember the room from an earlier visit to Hue. I'm in the Palace of Perfect Peace in the Forbidden City.

Cowboy punches my arm. "Okay, Joker, stop acting. We know you're not dead."

I sit up. I'm on a canvas med-evac stretcher. "There it is. I did it! Number one! I got my first heart."

Rafter Man says, "A Purple Heart?"

Cowboy laughs. "Tough titty, you poge. No heart."

I pat myself with my hands. "The hell you say. Where am I hit?"

Rafter Man says, "You been out for hours. Doc Jay said you got blown up by a B-40. A rocket-propelled grenade. But you only got the concussion. Some other guy got the shrapnel."

"Well," I say, "that sounds like a lifer-type thing to do."

Animal Mother grunts and spits. Animal Mother

spits a lot because he thinks it makes him look tough. "Lifers never get wasted. Just the ones I frag, that's all."

Donlon takes a step toward Animal Mother. Donlon is glaring at Animal Mother. Donlon starts to say something, then decides against it.

Rafter Man says, "Doc Jay gave you some morphine. You were trying to punch him out."

"There it is," I say. "I'm mean, even when I'm unconscious. But that's some very good shit, that morphine."

Cowboy pushes his gray Marine-issue glasses up on his nose. "I could use a hit of something myself. I wish we had time to smoke some grass."

I say, "Hey, bro, who's on your program?"

Cowboy shakes his head. "Mr. Shortround is KIA." Cowboy pulls a red bandanna from his back pocket and wipes his grimy face. "The platoon radioman was down. Some redneck from Alabama. I forget his name. Took a sniper round through the knee. The Skipper went out to get him. A frag got him. A frag got them both. At least . . ." Cowboy turns to look at Animal Mother. "At least, that's how Mother tells it, and he was walking point."

I shake the cobwebs out of my head and pick up my gear. "Where's my Mattel?"

Cowboy hands me a grease gun. "Your Mattel got wasted. Use this." He hands me a canvas bag containing half-a-dozen grease-gun magazines.

I check out the grease gun. "This thing is obsolete."

Cowboy shrugs. "I souvenired it off a wasted tanker." Cowboy scratches his face. "I got a new K-bar. And I souvenired Mr. Shortround's pistol."

"Where's Craze?"

Cowboy leads me outside to a long row of body bags and ponchos stuffed with human junk.

We stand over Craze as Cowboy says, "Craze did a John Wayne. He finally went berserk. Shot BB's at a gook machine gun. The BB's bounced off the gook gunners. You should have seen it. Craze was laughing like a happy little kid. Then that slope machine gun blew him away."

I nod. "Anybody else?"

Cowboy checks his weapon, snaps the bolt to see that it's working smoothly. "T.H.E. Rock. A sniper. Popped his head off. I'll have to tell you about it. Right now we got a job to do. We got to find that sniper. I'm personally going to waste that gook son-of-a-bitch. T.H.E. Rock was the first guy to get wasted after I took the squad. He's my responsibility."

Alice double-times up the road. "That sniper is still there. You can't see him, but he's there."

Cowboy doesn't say anything; he's looking at the long row of body bags. He takes a few steps. I walk along with him.

Mr. Shortround doesn't look like an officer anymore. He's naked, lying facedown on a bloody poncho. His skin is yellow. His eyes are dry in their sockets. Dead, Mr. Shortround is just another meat-bag with a hole in it.

Cowboy looks down at Mr. Shortround. He takes off his muddy Stetson.

Donlon steps up to Mr. Shortround. There are tears in Donlon's eyes. He fumbles with his handset. Donlon says, "We're mean Marines, sir." He hurries away, fumbling with the handset.

Alice walks up to the row of body bags and kicks Mr. Shortround's corpse. "Go easy, bro."

The squad files by.

I kneel. I fold the poncho over Mr. Shortround's small body. I feel a great need to say something to the green plastic lump with the human feet. I say, "Well, you're short, sir."

I think about what I have just said and I know that making a bad pun was a stupid thing to do. But then anything you could say to a dead officer who was killed by one of his own men would have to be pretty ridiculous.

Rafter Man and I double-time to catch up with the squad.

We hump past scented lotus ponds, through landscaped gardens, over bridges linking delicately structured pagodas.

All around the beautiful gardens invisible gunships rip into the peace and quiet like dogs fighting in a church.

Cowboy holds up his right hand. The squad stops. Alice aims an index finger at a street of big mansions.

Cowboy looks at me, then at the squad. Cowboy pulls me aside. We walk ahead for a few steps. "That sniper opened up on us in a gook graveyard. Some guys in One-One told us they found gold bars in the Emperor's palace. They had all they could hump, so we was going to souvenir the rest." Cowboy wipes sweat from his eyes. "The Rock was walking point. The sniper shot the Rock's foot off. Shot it off. The Hardass Squad went out to get him, one at a time. That sniper shot all their feet off. We were hiding behind graves, those old round graves like baseball mounds, and we had nine grunts down in the street. . . ." Cowboy pulls a red bandanna from his back pocket and wipes his sweaty face. "Mr. Shortround wouldn't let us go get them. It made him sick, but he held us back. Then the sniper started shooting off fingers, toes, ears—everything. The guys in the road were crying and begging and we were all growling like animals, but Mr. Shortround held us back. Then Animal Mother started to go for them and the Skipper grabbed Animal Mother's collar and hit him in the face. Animal Mother was so mad I thought he was going to kill us all. But before he could do anything the sniper started putting rounds into the guys in the street. He didn't miss more than a couple of times. He popped T.H.E. Rock's head off and then he put a round through each guy's head. They were all moaning and praying and then it was quiet and they were dead and it was like we were dead too. . . ."

I don't know what to say.

Cowboy spits, his face a sweaty stone. "After the NVA pulled out, the lifers sent in the Arvin Black Panthers to take the Forbidden City. Shit. Nothing left but rear guard squads. We stomped the NVA and they stomped us and then the lifers send in the Arvins, like the goddamn Arvins did it. Mr. Shortround said it was their country, said we was only helping out, said it would boost the morale of the Vitnamese people. Well, fuck the Vietnamese people. The horrible hogs in hard, hungry Hotel Company ran up an American flag. Like on Iwo Jima. But some poge officers ordered them to take it down. The snuffies had to run up the stinking Vietnamese flag, which is yellow, which is the right color for these chickenshit people. We're getting slaughtered in this city. And we can't even run up a fucking flag. I just can't hack this shit, bro. My job is to get my people

109

back to the World in one piece." Cowboy coughs, spits, wipes his nose with the back of his hand. "Under fire, these are the best human beings in the world. All they need is for somebody to throw hand grenades at them for the rest of their lives. . . . These guys depend on me. I can't send my people out to get that sniper, Joker. I might lose the whole squad."

I wait until I'm sure that Cowboy has finished talking and then I say, "That sounds like a personal problem to me, Cowboy. I can't tell you what to do. If I was a human being instead of a Marine, maybe I'd know." I scratch my armpit. "You're the honcho. You're the sergeant around here and you give the orders. You make the decisions. I could never do it. I could never run a rifle squad. Never happen, bro. I just don't have the balls."

Cowboy thinks about it. Then he grins. "You're right, Joker. You shitbird. You're right. I've got to get my program squared away. I wish Gunny Gerheim was here. He'd know what to do." Cowboy thinks about it. He grins. "Shit." He walks back to the squad. "Moving. . . ."

The squad hesitates. Crazy Earl has always been the one to say what is.

Animal Mother stands up. He sets his M-60 machine gun into his hip. He doesn't speak. He looks at the dirty faces of the squad. He moves out.

The squad collects its gear and gets to its feet.

Cowboy waves his hand and Mother takes the point.

We are discussing the best way to search the street house to house when a tank rumbles up.

Donlon says, "Hey, a tank! We can get it to—"

"*No*," says Cowboy. "Number ten! We don't need any help."

"That's affirmative," says Animal Mother.

I say, "A tank could flush him for us, Cowboy. Think about it. We can't budge gook grunts without supporting arms."

Cowboy shrugs. "Oh, to hell with it."

I double-time down the road to meet the tank. I run past heaps of rubble which were houses yesterday, bricks and stones and shattered wood today.

The tank jerks to a halt. The turret whirs. The big ninety-millimeter gun locks on me. For a long moment I think that the tank is going to blow me away.

The top half of the blond tank commander appears in the turret hatch. The lieutenant is wearing a flak jacket and an olive-drab football helmet with a microphone that protrudes over his lips. He is a mechanical centaur, half man, half tank.

I point out the mansions and I explain about the sniper, about how the sniper wasted our bro and all that good shit.

Cowboy comes over and tells the lieutenant to "wait one" and then to start wasting the mansions, one after another.

The blond tank commander is silent. He gives us a thumbs-up.

Cowboy sends Lance Corporal Stutten and his fire team around behind the row of mansions.

Animal Mother sets up his M-60 on a low wall and opens fire, raking the mansions at random. Every fifth round is a tracer.

The tank rolls up to the first mansion.

The rest of us double-time down an alley and cross the road a hundred yards down the street, at the end of the row of mansions.

At the opposite end of the street sits the tank. The tank fires a round of high explosives. The upper story of the first house is blown apart. The roof collapses.

Animal Mother continues to fire from his position near the tank.

Cowboy double-times to the first house at our end of the street. He steps carefully to the rear corner of the house, peeks around the corner. Cowboy waits for Lance Corporal Stutten to pop a green smoke as a signal that his fire team is in position as a blocking force.

We wait.

When green smoke begins to pour from a drainage ditch behind the first house at the far end of the street Cowboy waves his hand and we all open fire at the first house at our end of the street. One at a time, we run across the street to the first house, joining Cowboy.

Cowboy waves his hand around the corner and Lance Corporal Stutten's fire team opens up with their weapons on full automatic, pouring hundreds of high-velocity copper-jacketed bullets into the rear of the first house at their end of the street.

Animal Mother continues to chew up the fronts of all the mansions with his black steel machine gun.

The tank fires a second round. The ground floor of the first house is blown apart. The tank grinds forward twenty yards, stops, fires again. The second story of the second house explodes.

Cowboy leads us into the mansion at our end of the street. Inside, we leapfrog from corner to corner. Cowboy pops a frag and underhands it into somebody's kitchen. The detonation rocks the whole house, numbs our ears.

Rafter Man steps forward. He gestures to Cowboy, jerks his thumb at the ceiling. Cowboy holds up a circled thumb and index finger, "okay." Rafter Man pops a frag and pitches it up a stairwell to the second story. The explosion splits the plaster over our heads.

Outside, up the street, the tank fires again.

Cowboy punches me in the chest with his knuckles. Then he punches Rafter Man and Alice. He aims his right index finger at Donlon, then at the deck. Donlon nods and begins to silently point out the positions he wants the men in the squad to take.

Cowboy waves his hand and we follow him up the stairs.

Upstairs, Alice kicks out a window and we all hop out onto the roof.

The tank is two houses away. It fires.

We drop our gear and jump the six-foot chasm between houses.

On the roof of the second house Cowboy stands up and signals Lance Corporal Stutten, who waves back with his poncho. Bullets from Lance Corporal Stutten's fire team stop hitting the rear of the house we're standing on.

I double-time to the front of the house and I wave to Animal Mother. Bullets from Animal Mother's machine gun stop hitting the front of the house.

The tank fires. The shell bursts. Shrapnel whines over us.

We converge on a skylight. I drop a frag through the glass.

The grenade explodes in an invisible room below. Concussion shatters the skylight.

We drop through the ragged rectangular hole into somebody's library. Shrapnel has mangled leatherbound books. I pick up a small leatherbound book for a souvenir. The author is Jules Verne; the title is in French. I stuff the book into my thigh pocket and reach to the front of my flak jacket for another grenade.

We work our way through the house, fragging every hallway, every room. But we can't find the sniper.

The tank fires into the second story of the house next door.

I say, "No time."

Cowboy shrugs. "He wasted the Rock."

I take a few steps down the stairs. Cowboy holds up his hand. "Listen."

Animal Mother's M-60 is ripping up the roof over our heads.

I say, "Is Mother *dinky-dow*? Crazy?"

Cowboy shakes his head. "No. Mother is a prick, but he's a good grunt."

We run back to the library.

We drag a heavy antique desk to the ruined skylight and Cowboy climbs up onto it and lifts himself back onto the roof.

The crack of a Simonov sniper's carbine pierces the muted rhythm of Mother's machine gun.

Cowboy falls back through the skylight. Alice, who has climbed up onto the desk, catches Cowboy and eases him down to the desktop.

I pop a frag. I climb up onto the desk and take hold of the roof with my left hand. I let the spoon fly. The spoon *phinnnnings* away and rattles across the floor. I hold the sweaty green oval for three seconds and, lifting myself up, I flip it up and back so that it rolls across the roof directly over us. The frag bursts, spraying seven hundred and fifty pieces of steel wire across the roof. The ceiling splits. Alice hugs Cowboy. Plaster and splintered wood bounce off my helmet.

Rafter Man jumps up onto the desk and lifts himself up onto the roof.

Surprised, I pull myself up after him.

The tank fires into the ground floor of the house next door.

Rafter Man and I crawl on our bellies on the roof.

Behind us, Alice lifts Cowboy over his head like a wrestler, deposits him gently upon the roof. Then Alice climbs up. He picks Cowboy up in his arms as though Cowboy were an oversized baby.

Doc Jay calls to us from the roof of the first house.

Alice pulls a tent rope from a thigh pocket and ties it under Cowboy's arms. He flips the other end of the rope to Doc Jay. Doc Jay gets a good grip on the rope and braces himself as Alice lowers Cowboy into the chasm between the houses. Doc Jay pulls in the slack as Cowboy falls. Cowboy's limp body swings over and thuds into the wall beneath Doc Jay's feet. Doc Jay grits his teeth, pulls Cowboy up. Alice looks back at me, but I wave him on. He leaps over to the first house.

Doc Jay gathers up all of our gear and Alice throws Cowboy over his shoulder and they start back down.

Rafter Man has crawled up to the crest of the roof. He peeks over the crest.

*Bang.* A hiss.

I crawl up beside Rafter Man. I take a peek. From

behind a low chimney at the opposite corner of the roof a thin black line protrudes.

We hear the incredibly loud clanking of the tank as it rolls on the street below. It stops.

Animal Mother and Lance Corporal Stutten stop firing.

"Let's go," I say. I grab Rafter's shoulder. "The tank can waste the gook."

Rafter Man doesn't look at me. He pulls away.

I turn away and I duck walk to the edge of the roof. I stand up and am about to jump across when the house explodes beneath me.

I fall on my back.

The sniper is moving.

Rafter Man jumps over the crest of the roof and slides down the incline on his ass.

I try to stand up. But all of my bones have shifted one inch to the left.

Suddenly a foot steps on my chest, pinning me. The sniper looks down, surprised. The sniper sees that I'm helpless, glances back at Rafter Man, gets ready to jump across to the other roof.

Rafter Man runs back up the incline and slides back down on his ass, ten yards away.

I reach for my grease gun.

The sniper turns toward Rafter Man and raises her SKS carbine.

The sniper is the first Victor Charlie I've seen who was not dead, captured, or far, far away. She is a child, no more than fifteen years old, a slender Eurasian angel with dark, beautiful eyes, which, at the same time, are the hard eyes of a grunt. She's not quite five feet tall. Her hair is long and black and shiny, held together by rawhide cord tied in a bow. Her shirt and shorts are mustard-colored khaki and look new. Slung diagonally across her chest, separating her small breasts, is a white cloth tube fat with sticky reddish rice. Her B. F. Goodrich sandals have been cut from discarded tires. Around her tiny waist hangs a web belt from which dangle homemade hand grenades with hollow wooden handles, made by stuffing black powder into Coca-Cola cans, a knife for cleaning fish, and six canvas pouches containing banana clips for the AK-47 assault rifle slung on her back.

*Bang.* Rafter Man is firing his M-16. *Bang. Bang.*

The sniper lowers her weapon. She looks at Rafter Man. She looks at me. She tries to raise her weapon.

*Bang. Bang. Bang. Bang. Bang.* Bullets shock flesh. Rafter Man is firing. Rafter Man's bullets are punching the life out of the sniper.

The sniper falls off the roof.

The tank fires into the ground floor beneath us. The house shakes.

I stand up. I feel like a dead man's shit. I walk to the front of the house. I wave to the blond tank commander. He swings a fifty-caliber machine gun around and aims it at me. I step into full view on the edge of the roof. I wave an "all clear."

The tank commander gives me a thumbs-up.

I pop a green smoke grenade and I drop it on the roof.

I limp over to the skylight and I climb back down into the library.

Rafter Man has already jumped into the library and is running down the shrapnel-scarred stairs.

Down on the street I watch as the tank rolls up to the last house still standing. I wave another "all clear" and the tank commander gives me another smile and another thumbs-up and then the tank fires, blasting the top floor. It fires again, blasting the ground floor.

The tank commander's great mechanical body grumbles contentedly and rumbles away.

Cowboy double-times to meet me. He punches me on the arm. "Look!" Cowboy touches his right ear, carefully. "Look!" There's a neat little round hole through his right ear and a semicircular nick on the top of his left ear. "See? A cheap Heart! The round went through the helmet from behind, spun all the way around my head, then came out and hit me in the arm. . . ." Cowboy holds up his right forearm, which has already been bandaged. "Did you see that tank? Was that tank bad? What a honey."

Doc Jay catches up to Cowboy, grabs him roughly, pushes him down. Cowboy sits on a splintered tree stump while Doc Jay tears the waxy brown wrapper off a compress bandage and ties the bandage around Cowboy's bloody head.

Alice and I walk around to the rear of the house.

We find Rafter Man standing over the sniper, drinking a bottle of Coca-Cola. Rafter Man grins. He says, "Things go better with coke."

Animal Mother walks up and Rafter Man says, "Look at her! Look at her!"

We all stand over the sniper. The sniper is drawing her breath with great effort. Guts that look like colorful plastic have squirted out through bullet holes. The back of the sniper's right leg and her right buttock have been torn off. She grits her teeth and then makes a sound like a dog that has been run over.

Lance Corporal Stutten leads his fire team to the sniper. "Look at that," says Lance Corporal Stutten. "It's a girl. She's all busted up."

"Look at her!" Rafter Man is saying. He struts around the moaning lump of torn meat. "Look at her! Am I bad? Am I a menace? Am I a life *taker?* Am I a heart *breaker?*"

Alice kneels and unbuckles the sniper's web belt and jerks it from under her body. The sniper whimpers. She speaks to us in French. Alice tosses the bloody belt to Rafter Man.

The sniper begins to pray in Vietnamese.

Rafter Man asks, "What's she's saying?"

I shrug. "What difference does it make?"

Animal Mother spits. "It's gonna get dark. We better hump back to the company area."

I say, "What about the gook?"

"Fuck her," says Animal Mother. "Let her rot."

"We can't just leave her here," I say.

Animal Mother takes a giant step toward me, puts his face up close to mine. "Hey, asshole, Cowboy is down. You're fresh out of friends, motherfucker. I'm running this squad. I was a platoon sergeant before they busted me. I say we leave the gook for the mother-loving rats."

Rafter Man is buckling on his NVA belt. The belt has a dull-silver buckle with a star engraved in the center. "Joker is a sergeant."

Animal Mother is surprised. He stares at Rafter Man, then at me. Then: "That don't cut no shit out here. This is the field, motherfucker. You ain't a grunt. You don't pack the gear to be a grunt. You want to fuck with me? Huh? You want to throw some hands?"

I say, "I wouldn't run this squad for a million dollars. I'm just saying that we can't leave the gook like this."

"I don't care," says Animal Mother. "Go on and waste her."

I say, "No. Not me."

"Then we saddle up and move . . . *now.*"

I look at the sniper. She whimpers. I try to decide what I would want if I were down, half dead, hurting bad, surrounded by my enemies. I look into her eyes, trying to find the answer. She sees me. She recognizes me—I am the one who will end her life. We share a bloody intimacy. As I lift my grease gun she is praying in French. I jerk the trigger. *Bang.* One round enters the sniper's left eye and as the bullet exits it tears off the back of her head.

The squad is silent.

Then Alice grunts, flashes a big grin. "Man, you are one hard dude. How come you ain't a grunt?"

Cowboy and Doc Jay are standing beside me.

Cowboy says, "Mother, I'm serviceable. Joker, that's a well done. You're hard."

Animal Mother spits. He takes a step, kneels, zips out his machete. With one powerful blow he chops off her head. He picks the head up by its long black hair and holds it high. He laughs and says, "Rest in pieces, bitch." And he laughs again. He walks around and sticks the bloody ball of gore into all our faces. "Hard? *Now* who's hard? Now who's hard, motherfuckers?"

Cowboy looks at Animal Mother and sighs. "Joker is hard, Mother. You . . . you're just mean."

Animal Mother pauses, spits, throws the head into a ditch.

Cowboy says, "Let's move. We done our job."

Animal Mother picks up his M-60 machine gun, lays it across his shoulders, struts over to me. He smiles. "You know, Shortround never did see the frag that wasted him, that little kike." Animal Mother unhooks a hand grenade from the front of his flak jacket and pushes it into my chest—*hard*. Mother looks around, then smiles at me again. "Nobody shits on the Animal, motherfucker. *No*body."

I hook the grenade onto my flak jacket.

Alice picks up the sniper's rifle. "Hey, number one souvenir!"

Rafter Man is standing over the sniper's decapitated corpse. He aims his M-16 and fires a long burst of automatic fire into the body. Then he says, "That's *mine*, Alice." He takes the SKS from Alice and examines it closely. He looks down and admires his new belt. "I shot her first, Joker. She'd have died. That's one confirmed for me."

I say, "Sure, Rafter. You wasted her."

Rafter Man says, "I did. I wasted her. I fucking blew her away." He looks at his NVA rifle belt again. He holds up the SKS. "Wait until Mr. Payback sees *this!*"

Alice is down on his knees beside the corpse. With his machete he chops off the sniper's feet. He puts the feet into his blue canvas shopping bag. He chops off the sniper's finger and takes her gold ring.

We wait while Rafter Man takes photographs of the dead gook and we wait while Alice takes photographs of Rafter Man posing with his SKS set in his hip and his foot on the mutilated remains of the enemy sniper.

Then, as we're moving out, Rafter Man sees a reflection of his face in the jagged teeth of a shattered window, sees the new smile upon his face. Rafter Man stares at himself for a long time and then, dropping the carbine, Rafter Man just walks off down the road, not looking back, not responding to our questions.

Cowboy waves his hand and we move out. Nobody says anything about Rafter Man.

We hump back to the Forbidden City and set in for the night.

I mark the short-timer's calendar on my flak jacket— fifty-five days and a wake-up left in country.

Later, in the dark, Rafter Man comes back.

The fighting continues all around us all night, sputters of violence here and there, a mortar round, a curse, a scream.

We sleep like babies.


The sun that rises in Hue on the morning of February 25, 1968, illuminates a dead city. United States Marines have liberated Hue to the ground. Here, in the heart of the ancient imperial capital of Viet Nam, a living shrine to the Vietnamese people on both sides, green Marines in the green machine have liberated a cherished past. Green Marines in the green machine have shot the bones of sacred ancestors. Wise, like Solomon, we have converted Hue into rubble in order to save it.


The next morning Delta Six cuts us some slack and we spend the day hunting gold bars in the emperor's palace.

We enter the throne room of the old emperors. The throne is blood red, studded with inlaid mirrors.

I wish I could live in the Imperial Palace. Bright

pieces of porcelain make the walls vivid. The roof is orange tile. There are stone dragons, ceramic urns, brass cranes standing on the backs of turtles, and many other fine objects of undetermined origin and function but obviously of great value and great beauty and very old.

I walk out into the emperor's magnificent garden. I find Alice and Rafter Man looking at some crispy critters. It's impossible to determine which army the men were from. Napalm leaves less than bones. I say, "The aroma of roasted flesh is, admittedly, an acquired taste."

Alice laughs. "This is such a fucking waste. I mean, this place is like a magic temple, you know? The gooks love this place. Blowing it away is like, oh, blowing away the White House. Except that nobody gives a shit about the White House and this place is ten times as old."

I shrug.

"It's crazy," Alice says. "It's just plain fucking crazy. I wish I was back in the World."

I say, "No, back in the World is the crazy part. This, all this world of shit, this is real."

Cowboy comes around later and says that Delta's company commander has passed the word to regroup on the beach at the Strawberry Patch.

We march. We look at the rubble we have made. We get tired of looking at it; there's so much of it.


Twilight.

What's left of Delta Company, 1st Battalion, Fifth Marine Regiment, First Marine Division, is sprawled all over the beach down by the River of Perfumes. The bearded grunts are sleeping, cooking chow, brag-

123

ging, comparing souvenirs, and reenacting every moment of the battle, real and imagined, every man a hero beyond belief.

The Lusthog Squad is wasted. We have nailed our names into the pages of history enough for today. Canteens come out. It's too hot to cook so we eat cold C's.

Some of the guys are getting to their feet.

Donlon stands up, shouts, "LOOK!"

Five hundred yards north there is an island in the River of Perfumes. On the island a semicircle of miniature tanks is converging upon a frantic colony of ants. The ants drop their gear and sling their AK-47 assault rifles over their backs and they jump into the river. The ants swim for it.

All of the tanks open fire with ninety-millimeter shells and with fifty-caliber machine guns.

Some of the ants sink.

Cobra gunships buzz out of a horizon that is the color of lead and swoop in for the kill.

The ants swim faster.

The hovering gunships chop up the brown water with their machine guns.

The ants swim, dive, or, in their panic, drown.

Delta Company gets onto its feet.

Three Cobra gunships zoom down to within a few yards of the river and the helmeted door gunners machine-gun the ants as they flop in the water, trapped in a syncopated hurricane of hot air beating down from the swirling rotor blades, trapped in the water while their red life runs out through bullet holes.

Only one ant reaches the river bank. The ant opens fire at the gunships as they hover over the water like monsters feeding.

Someone says, "See that shit? He's hard-core."

One gunship detaches itself from the blood feast and skims across the River of Perfumes. The chopper drops bullets all over the beach, all around the ant.

The ant runs off the beach.

The gunship zooms back to feed on the ants in the water.

The ant runs out onto the beach and opens fire.

The gunship banks sharply and comes in low, rockets swooshing from under its belly and machine guns chattering.

Again, the ant runs off the beach.

The gunship is halfway back to the ants in the water when the ant on the beach reappears and opens fire.

This time the gunship pilot brings his ship in low enough to decapitate the ant with the chopper's skids. The gunship fires.

The ant fires.

Machine-gun bullets knock the ant over.

The gunship swings around to verify that it is a confirmed kill.

As machine-gun bullets snap into the wet sand, the ant stands up, aims its tiny AK-47 assault rifle, and fires a thirty-round magazine on full automatic.

The Cobra gunship explodes, splits open like a bloated green egg. The gutted carcass of aluminum and plexiglass bounces along, suspended in the air, burning, trailing black smoke. And then it falls.

The flaming chopper hits the river and the flowing water sucks it down.

The ant does not move. The ant fires another magazine on full automatic. The ant is shooting at the sky.

Tired of firing into floating corpses, the remaining two gunships attack.

The ant walks off the beach.

The gunships hit the beach and sand dunes with every weapon they've got. They circle and circle and circle like predatory birds. Then, out of ammunition and out of fuel, they buzz straight into the horizon and vanish.

Delta Company applauds and cheers and whistles. "Get some! Number one! Out-fucking-sanding! Payback is a motherfucker!"

Alice says, "That guy was a grunt."

While we wait for the gunboats to come and take us back across the River of Perfumes we talk about how the NVA grunt was one hell of a hard individual and about how it would be okay if he came to America and married all our sisters and about how we all hope that he will live to be a hundred years old because the world will be diminished when he's gone.

The next morning, Rafter Man and I get the map coordinates of a mass grave from some green ghouls and we hump over to the site to get Captain January his atrocity photographs.

The mass grave smells really bad—the odor of blood, the stink of worms, decayed human beings. The Arvin snuffies doing the digging in a school yard have all tied olive-drab skivvy shirts around their faces, but casualties due to uncontrollable puking are heavy.

We see corpses of Vietnamese civilians who have been buried alive, faces frozen in mid-scream, hands like claws, the fingernails bloody and caked with damp earth. All of the dead people are grinning that hideous, joyless grin of those who have heard the joke, of those who have seen the terrible secrets of the earth. There's even the corpse of a dog which Victor Charlie could not separate from its master.

There are no corpses with their hands tied behind their backs. However, the green ghouls assure us that they have seen such corpses elsewhere. So I borrow some demolition wire from the Arvin snuffies and, crushing the stiff bodies with my knee until dry bones crack, I bind up a family, assembled at random from the multitude—a man, his wife, a little boy, a little girl, and, of course, their dog. As a final touch I wire the dog's feet together.

Noon at the MAC-V compound. We say good-bye to Cowboy and to the Lusthog Squad.

Cowboy has found a stray puppy and is carrying the bony little animal inside his shirt. Cowboy says to me, "Keep your ass down, bro. Scuttlebutt is, the Lusthog Squad is headed up to Khe Sanh, a very hairy area. But no sweat; we can hack it. And maybe they got some horses up there. So if you ever feel hard enough to be a real Marine, a grunt, bop up to see us."

I pet Cowboy's puppy. "Never happen. But you take care, you piece of shit. We've got a date with your sister I don't want to miss."

Rafter Man says good-bye to Alice and to the other guys in Cowboy's squad. He shakes hands with Cowboy and pets Cowboy's puppy. In my best John Wayne voice I say, "See you later, Mother."

Animal Mother says, "Not if I see you first."

Rafter Man and I ditty-bop down Route One, south, toward Phu Bai. We hump in crushing heat for hours, looking for a ride. But the sun is without mercy and there are no convoys in sight.

We sit in the shade by the road. "It's hot," I say. "It's very hot. Wish that old *mamasan* was here. I'd souvenir beaucoup money for one Coke. . . ."

Rafter Man stands up. "No sweat. I can find her. . . ." Rafter Man ditty-bops into the road.

I start to say something about how it might be a good idea for us to stay together. There are still plenty of NVA stragglers in the area. "Rafter . . ." But then I remember that Rafter Man has got his first confirmed kill. Rafter Man can take care of himself.

The deck trembles. A tank? I look up, but I can't see anything on the road. Yet nothing on earth sounds as big as a tank, nothing produces that terrible rumble of metal like a tank. It shakes my bones. I jump up, weapon ready. I look up and down the road. Nothing. But all around me is the clamor of rolling iron and the odor of diesel fuel.

Rafter Man is walking across the road. He does not hear the invisible tank. He does not feel the mechanical earthquake.

I double-time after him. "Rafter!"

Rafter Man turns around. He grins. And then we both see it. The tank is an object of heavy metal forged from a cold shadow, a ghost with substance. The black mechanical phantom comes for us, dark ectoplasm rolling in the sun. The blond tank commander stands in the turret hatch, staring straight ahead and into the beyond, laughing.

Rafter Man turns around.

I say, "Don't move."

But Rafter looks at me, panic on his face.

I grab his shoulder.

Rafter Man pulls away and runs.

The tank is bearing down on me. I don't move.

The tank swerves, misses me, roars past like a big iron dragon. The tank runs over Rafter Man and crushes him beneath its steel treads. And then it's gone.

Rafter Man lies on his back in the dirt, a crushed dog spilling out of its skin. Rafter Man looks at me the way he looked at me that day at the Freedom Hill PX on Hill 327 in Da Nang. His eyes are begging me for an explanation.

Rafter Man has been cut in half just below his new NVA rifle belt. His intestines are pink rope all over the deck. He is trying to pull himself back in, but it doesn't work. His guts are wet and slippery and he can't hold them in. He tries to reinsert his spilling guts back into his severed torso. He tries very hard to keep the dirt off of his intestines as he works.

Rafter Man stops trying to save himself and, instead, just stares at me with an expression that might be found on the face of a person who wakes up with a dead bird in his mouth.

"Sarge . . ."

"Don't call me 'Sarge'." I say.

I kneel down and pick up Rafter's black-body Nikon. I say, "I'll tell Mr. Payback about your belt and about your SKS. . . ." I want so much to cry, but I can't cry—I'm too tough.

I stop talking to Rafter Man because Rafter Man is dead. Talking to dead people is not a healthy habit for a living person to cultivate and lately I have been talking to dead people quite a lot. I guess I've been talking to dead people ever since I made my first confirmed kill. After my first confirmed kill, talking to corpses began to make more sense than talking to people who had not yet been wasted.

In Viet Nam you see corpses almost every day. At first you try to ignore them. You don't want people to think you're curious. Nobody wants to admit that corpses are not old hat to them; nobody wants to be a New Guy. So you see lumps of dirty rags. And after a while you begin to notice that the lumps of dirty rags have arms and legs and heads. And faces.

The first time I saw a corpse, back when I was a New Guy, I wanted to vomit, just like in the movies. The corpse was an NVA grunt who died in a great orange ball of jellied gasoline near Con Thien. The napalm left a crumbled heap of ashes in the fetal position. His mouth was open. His charred fingers were covering his eyes.

The second time I really looked at a corpse I was embarrassed. The corpse was an old Vietnamese woman with teeth which had turned black after a lifetime of chewing betel nuts. The woman had been hit by something bigger than small-arms fire. She was killed in a crossfire between ROK Marines and NVA grunts in Hoi An. She seemed so exposed in death, so vulnerable.

My third corpse was a decapitated Marine. I stumbled over him on an operation in the A Shau valley. My reaction was curiosity. I wondered what the rounds had felt like as they entered his body, what his last thought was, what his last sound was at the moment of impact. I marveled at the ultimate power of death. A big strong American boy, so vibrant and red-blooded, had become within minutes a yellow lump of inflexible meat. And I understood that my own weapon could do this dark magic thing to any human being. With my automatic rifle I could knock the life out of any enemy with just the slightest pressure of one finger. And, knowing that, I was less afraid.

The fourth corpse is the last one I remember. After that they're blurred together, a mountain of faceless dead. But I think that the fourth corpse was the old *papasan* in the conical white hat I saw on Route One. The old man had been run over by a six-by as he squatted in the road taking a shit. All I remember is that when I marched by, flies exploded off the old man like pieces of shrapnel.

I got my first confirmed kill with India Three-Five.

I was writing a feature article about how the grunts at the Rockpile on Route Nine had to sweep the road for mines every morning before any traffic could use the road. There was a fat gunny who insisted on walking point with a metal detector. The fat gunny wanted to protect his people. He believed that fate killed the careless. He stepped on an antitank mine. A man is not supposed to be heavy enough to detonate an antitank mine, but the gunny was pretty fat.

The earth opened up and hell came out with a roar that jarred my bones. The fat gunny was launched into the clean blue sky, green and round and loose-jointed like a broken doll. I watched the fat gunny float up to heaven and then a wall of heat slammed into me and I collided with the deck.

The fat gunny floated back to earth.

Although shrapnel had stung my face and peppered my flak jacket, I was not afraid. I was very calm. From the moment the mine detonated I knew I was a dead man, and there was nothing I could do.

Behind me a man was cursing. The man was a Navy corpsman. The corpsman's right hand had been split open and he was holding his fingers together with his good hand and cursing and yelling for a corpsman.

Then I understood that the "shrapnel" I'd felt had only been shattered gravel.

Grunts from the security squad were crawling into the bushes, turning outboard, weapons ready.

Still confused about why I was still alive I got to my feet and double-timed to the little pit that had been torn into the road by the explosion.

Two grunts were double-timing across a meadow toward a treeline. I followed them, my finger on the trigger of my M-16, eager to pour invisible darts of destruction into the shadows.

The two grunts and I ran and ran until we passed through the treeline and emerged on the edge of a vast rice paddy. There the fat gunny was floating on his back in the shallow water, surrounded by dark pieces of do-it-yourself fertilizer.

The grunts spread a poncho under him while I stood security. Both of the gunny's legs had been torn off at the pelvis. I saw one of his fat legs floating nearby so I picked it up out of the water and threw it in on top of him.

We all took hold of the poncho and started carrying the heavy load back to the road. I was breathing hard, and black anger was pounding inside my chest. I was watching the trees, hoping I'd see movement.

And then out of nowhere a man appeared, a tiny, ancient farmer who was at the same time ridiculous and dignified. The ancient farmer had a hoe on his shoulder and was wearing the obligatory conical white hat. His chest was bony and he looked so old. His sturdy legs were scarred. The ancient farmer didn't speak to us. He just stood there beside the trail with rice shoots in his hand, calm, his mind rehearsing the hard work he had to do that day.

The ancient farmer smiled. He saw the frantic children with their fat burden of death and he felt sorry for us. So he smiled to show that he understood what we were going through. Then my M-16 was vibrating and invisible metal missles were snapping through the ancient farmer's body as though he were a bag of dry sticks.

The ancient farmer looked at me. As he fell forward into the dark water his face was tranquil and I could see that he understood.

After my first confirmed kill I began to understand that it was not necessary to understand. What you do, you become. The insights of one moment are blotted out by the events of the next. And no amount of insight could ever alter the cold, black fact of what I had done. I was caught up in a constricting web of darkness, and, like the ancient farmer, I was suddenly very calm, just as I had been calm when the mine detonated, because there was nothing I could do. I was defining myself with bullets; blood had blemished my Yankee Doodle dream that everything would have a happy ending, and that I, when the war was over, would return to hometown America in a white silk uniform, a rainbow of campaign ribbons across my chest, brave beyond belief, the military Jesus.

I think about my first kill for a long time. At twilight a corpsman appears. I explain to him that Marines never abandon their dead or wounded.

The corpsman looks at each of Rafter Man's pupils several times. "What?"

I shrug. I say. "Payback is a motherfucker."

"What?" The corpsman is confused. The corpsman is obviously a New Guy.

"Tanks for the memories . . ." I say, because I do not know how to tell him how I feel. You're a machine gunner who has come to the end of his last belt. You're waiting, staring out through the barbed wire at the little men who are assaulting your position. You see their tiny toy-soldier bayonets and their determined, eyeless faces, but you're a machine gunner who has come to the end of his last belt and there's nothing you can do. The little men are going to grow and grow and grow—illuminated by the fluid, ghostly fire of a star flare—and then they're going to run up over you and cut you up with knives. You see this. You know this. But you're a machine gunner who has come to the end of his last belt and there's nothing you can do. In their distant fury the little men are your brothers and you love them more than you love your friends. So you wait for the little men to come and you know you'll be waiting for them when they come because you no longer have anywhere else to go. . . .

The corpsman is confused. He does not understand why I'm smiling. "Are you okay, Marine?" Yes, he is a New Guy for sure.

I ditty-bop down the road. The corpsman calls after me. I ignore him.

A mile away from the place of fear I stick out my thumb.


I'm dirty, unshaven, and dead tired.

A Mighty Mite slams on its brakes. "MARINE!"

I turn, thinking I've got some slack, thinking I've got a ride.

A poge colonel pounces out of the jeep, marches up to face me. "MARINE!"

I think: Is that you, John Wayne? Is this me? "Aye-aye, sir."

"Corporal, don't you know how to execute a hand salute?"

"Yes, *sir*." I salute. I hold the salute until the poge colonel snaps his hand to his starched barracks cover and I hold the salute for an extra couple of seconds before cutting it away sharply. Now the poge colonel has been identified as an officer to any enemy snipers in the area.

"Corporal, don't you know how to stand to *attention?*"

Right away I start wishing I was back in the shit. In battles there are no police, only people who want to shoot you. In battles there are no poges. Poges try to kill you on the inside. Poges leave your body intact because your muscles are all they want from you anyway.

I stand to attention, wobbling slightly beneath the sixty pounds of gear I'm humping.

The poge colonel has a classic granite jaw. I'm sure that the Marine Corps must have a strict examination at the officers' candidate school at Quantico designed to eliminate all officer candidates who lack the granite jaw.

His jungle utilities are razor-creased, starched to the consistency of green armor. He executes a flawless Short Pause, a favorite technique of leaders of men, designed to inflict its victim with fatal insecurity. Having no desire to damage the colonel's self-confi-

135

dence, I respond with my best Parris Island rendition of I-am-only-an-enlisted-person-I-try-to-be-humble.

"Marine . . ." The colonel stands ramrod straight. This stance is the Air of Command, intended to intimidate me, despite the fact that I'm a foot taller and outweigh him by fifty pounds. The colonel investigates the underside of my chin. "Marine . . ." He likes that word. "What is that on your body armor, Marine?"

"Sir?"

The poge colonel stands on tiptoe. For a moment I'm afraid he's going to bite me in the neck. But he only wants to breathe on me. His smile is cold. His skin is too white. "Marine . . ."

"Sir?"

"I asked you a question."

"You mean this peace button, sir?"

"What is it?"

"A peace symbol, sir. . . ."

I wait patiently while the colonel tries to remember the "Maintaining Interpersonal Relationships with Subordinate Personnel" chapter of his OCS textbook.

The poge colonel continues to breathe all over my face. His breath smells of mint. Marine Corps officers are not allowed to have bad breath, body odor, acne pimples, nor holes in their underwear. Marine Corps officers are not allowed to have anything that has not been issued to them.

The colonel jabs my button with a forefinger, gives me a fairly decent Polished Glare. His blue eyes sparkle. "That's right, son, act innocent. But I *know* what that button means."

"Yes, *sir!*"

"It's a ban-the-bomb propaganda button. Admit it!"

"No, sir." I'm in real pain. The man who invented standing at attention obviously never humped any gear.

"Then what *does* it mean?"

"It's just a symbol for peace, sir."

"Oh, yeah?" He breathes faster, up close now, as though he can smell lies.

"Yes, Colonel, it's just—"

"MARINE!"

"AYE-AYE, SIR!"

"WIPE THAT SMILE OFF YOUR FACE!"

"AYE-AYE, SIR!"

The poge colonel moves around me, stalks me. "Do you call yourself a Marine?"

"Well . . ."

"WHAT?"

Crossed fingers, king's-X. "Yes, sir."

"Now seriously, son . . ." The colonel begins an excellent Fatherly Approach. "Just tell me who gave you that button. You can level with me. You can trust me. I only want to help you." The poge colonel smiles.

The colonel's smile is funny so I smile, too.

"Where did you get that button, Marine?" The colonel looks hurt. "Don't you love your country, son?"

"Well . . ."

"Do you believe that the United States should allow the Vietnamese to invade Viet Nam just because they live here?" The poge colonel is struggling to regain his composure. "Do you?"

My shoulders are about to fall off. My legs are falling asleep. "No, *sir*. We should bomb them back to the Stone Age . . . *sir*."

"Confess, Corporal, confess that you want peace."

I give him a Short Pause. "Doesn't the colonel want peace . . . sir?"

The colonel hesitates. "Son, we've all got to keep our heads until this peace craze blows over. All I have ever asked of my boys is that they obey my orders as they would obey the word of God."

"Is that a negative . . . sir?"

The poge colonel tries to think of some more inspiring things to say to me, but he has used them all up. So he says, "You can't wear that button, Marine. It's against regulations. Remove it immediately or you *will* be standing tall before the man."

Somewhere up in Heaven, where the streets are guarded by Marines, Jim Nabors, in his Gomer Pyle uniform, sings: *"From the halls of Montezuma . . . to the shores of Tripoli. . . ."*

"MARINE!"

"YES, SIR!"

"WIPE THAT SMILE OFF YOUR FACE!"

"AYE-AYE, SIR!"

"The Commandant has ordered us to protect freedom by allowing the Vietnamese to live like Americans all they want to. As long as Americans are in Viet Nam the Vietnamese will have the right to express their political convictions without fear of reprisal. So I will say it one more time, Marine, take off that peace button or I will give you a tour of duty in Portsmouth Naval Prison."

I stay at attention.

The poge colonel remains calm. "I am going to cut a new set of orders on you, Corporal. I am personally going to demand that your commanding officer shit-can you to the grunts. Show me your dogtags."

I dig out my dogtags and I tear off the green masking tape around them and the poge colonel writes my name, rank, and serial number into a little green notebook.

"Come with me, Marine," says the poge colonel, putting the little green notebook back into his pocket. "I want to show you something."

I step over to the jeep. The poge colonel pauses for dramatic effect, then pulls a poncho off a lump on the back seat. The lump is a Marine lance corporal in the fetal position. In the lance corporal's neck are punctures—many, many of them.

The poge colonel grins, bares his vampire fangs, takes step toward me.

I punch him in the chest with my wooden bayonet.

He freezes. He looks down at the wooden bayonet. He looks at the deck, then at the sky. Suddenly his wristwatch is very interesting. "I . . . uh . . . I've got no more time to waste on this unprofitable encounter . . . and get a haircut!"

I salute. The poge colonel returns my salute. We hold the salutes awkwardly while the colonel says, "Someday, Corporal, when you're a little older, you'll realize how naive—"

The poge colonel's voice breaks on "naive."

I grin. His eyes fall.

Both salutes cut away nicely.

"Good day, Marine," says the poge colonel. Then, armored in the dignity awarded him by Congress, the colonel marches back to his Mighty Mite, climbs in, and drives away with his bloodless lance corporal.

The poge colonel's Mighty Mite lays rubber—after all that talking he doesn't even give me a ride.

"YES, SIR!" I say. "IT IS A GOOD DAY, SIR!"

The war goes on. Bombs fall. Little ones.

An hour later a deuce-and-a-half slams on its brakes. I climb up into the cab with the driver.

During the bumpy ride back to Phu Bai the driver of the deuce-and-a-half tells me about a mathematical system he has devised which he will use to break the bank in Las Vegas as soon as he gets back to the World.

As the driver talks the sun goes down and I think: Fifty-four days and a wake-up.

I've got forty-nine days and a wake-up left in country when Captain January hands me a piece of paper. Captain January mumbles something about how he hopes I have good luck and then he goes to chow even though it's not chow time.

The piece of paper orders me to report for duty as a rifleman with Delta Company, One-Five, currently based at the Khe Sanh.

I say good-bye to Chili Vendor and Daytona Dave and Mr. Payback and I tell them that I'm glad to be a grunt because now I won't have to write captions for atrocity photographs they just file away or tell any more lies because there's nothing more the lifers can threaten me with. "What are they going to do—send me to Viet Nam?"

Delta Six cuts Cowboy a huss and I'm assigned to Cowboy's squad as the first fire team leader—the assistant squad leader—until I've got enough field experience to run my own rifle squad.

There it is.

I'm a grunt.

# GRUNTS

*Behold a Marine, a mere shadow and reminiscence of humanity, a man laid out alive and standing, buried under arms with funereal accompaniments. . . .*

THOREAU, *Civil Disobedience*

Rolling thunder.

Clouds float across the white moon, clouds like great metal ships. Black wings beating, enormous objects falling. Arc Light in the monsoon rain; an air strike in the dark. A flight of B-52 bombers circles Khe Sanh, sprinkling eggs of black iron. Each egg weighs two thousand pounds. Each egg knocks a hole into the cold earth, punches a crater into the constricting web of slit trenches that forty thousand determined little men have dug to within a hundred yards of our wire. Black and wet, the earth heaves up like the deck of a great ship, heaves up toward the droning death birds.

Even in the fury of aerial bombardment we sleep, shadows in the earth. We sleep in holes we have dug with entrenching tools. The holes are little graves and hold the rich, damp odor of the grave.

The monsoon rain is cold and heavy and is thrown all over the place by the wind. The wind has power. The wind roars, hisses, whispers seductively. The wind claws at the shelters we have constructed with ponchos and nylon cord and scraps of bamboo.

Raindrops thump my poncho like pebbles falling into a broken drum. Half asleep, my face pressed into my gear, I listen to the sounds of the horror that is everywhere, buried just beneath the surface of the earth. In my dreams of blood I make love to a skeleton. Bones click, the earth moves, my testicles explode.

Shrapnel bites my shelter. I wake up. I listen to the fading drone of the B-52's. I listen to the breathing of my squad of brothers, nightmare men in the dark.

Outside our wire an enemy grunt is screaming at invisible airplanes that have killed him.

I try to dream something beautiful. . . . My grandmother sits in a rocking chair on her front porch shooting Viet Cong who have stepped on her roses. She drinks the blood of a dragon from a black Coca-Cola bottle while Göring my mother with fat white breasts nurses me and drives Germany on and on, his words cut from the armor plate of a tank. . . .

I sleep on steel, my face on a pillow of blood. I bayonet teddy bear and I snore. Bad dreams are something you ate. So sleep, you mother.

The wind roars up under my shelter and rips the poncho off its bamboo frame, snapping the lines that secured it. Rain falls on me like a wave of icy black water.

An angry voice drifts in from beyond the wire. An enemy sergeant is saying dirty words I don't understand. An enemy sergeant has stumbled over a dead man in the dark. . . .

Night patrol.

In the predawn sky a little metal star goes nova—an illumination round.

Eating an early breakfast in the red slime of a slit trench at Khe Sanh. Yesterday I made myself a new stove by punching air holes into an empty C's can. Inside the stove, C-4 plastic explosive glows like a fragment of brimstone. Ham and mothers pop and bubble in another olive-drab can while I mix and stir with a white plastic spoon.

On the horizon, orange tracers stitch the night. Puff the Magic Dragon, "Spooky", a C-47 flying electric Gatling gun, is pouring three hundred rounds per minute into some gook's wet dreams.

Taste the ham and lima beans. Hot. Greasy. Smells like pig shit. With my bayonet I lift the full can off the stove. I anchor the can in red mud. I balance my mess cup over the flame and pour in a packet of powdered cocoa and then half a canteen of spring water. With some slack, hot chocolate dilutes the sour aftertaste of halazone purification tablets.

A Viet Cong rat attacks. Obviously, he intends to bring my breakfast under the influence of Communism.

This is a rat I know personally, so I cut him some slack and do not set him on fire with lighter fluid the way my bros and I have done with his relatives. I stomp my foot and the rat retreats into a shadow.

In the light of the flare my bros in the Lusthog Squad of Delta One-Five look like pale lizards. My bros look up at me with hard eyes. No slack. I gave them the finger. Their lizard eyes click back to their poker cards.

From his new strategic position, the Viet Cong rat stares back to assert his principles.

The illumination flare trembles, freezes Khe Sanh into a faded daguerreotype. Look at all the junk of modern war spilled across our dusty citadel, look at how bearded grunts hang on while the world spins and gravity cheats, look at the concrete bones of an old French outpost (patrolled at night by the ghosts of dead Legionnaires and by the Mongol horsemen of Genghis Khan)—see how the broken walls of the outpost are like rotting teeth, look out beyond our wire at a thousand acres of blasted moonscape, feel the cold hard terror and the calm of it.

During the past three months the rocky terrain around Khe Sanh has been pounded with the greatest volume of explosives in the history of war. Two hundred million pounds of bombs and whole catalogues of other weapons have torn and plowed the sterile red earth, have shattered boulders, have splintered and chewed the stumps of trees, have pockmarked the deck with craters big enough to be graves for tanks.

The flare floats down beneath a miniature parachute, swaying and squeaking, dripping sparks and hissing, until it hits the wire. Illumination dissolves.

In the darkness I am one with Khe Sanh—a living cell of this place—this erupted pimple of sandbags and barbed wire on a bleak plateau surrounded by the end of the world. In my guts I know that my body is one of the components of gristle and muscle and bone of Khe Sanh, a small American community pounded daily by one-hundred-and-fifty-two-millimeter artillery pieces firing from caves eleven kilometers away on Co Roc Ridge in Laos, pounded by fifteen hundred shells a day, pounded, pounded, pounded with brain-numbing regularity, an anthill beneath a sledgehammer.

Today I am feeling extra fine—I'm short. Twenty-two days and a wake-up left in country.

The Viet Cong rat crouches on a sandbag an inch from my elbow. I bend over and put his share of ham and mothers on the toe of my boot. The rat watches me with black bead eyes. Rats are little but they're smart. After the rat is satisfied I can be trusted, he jumps off the sandbag and into the slit trench. He hops up onto the toe of my boot. Eating, his cheeks are fat. He looks so very bad; he's beautiful.

Roll call.

The squad files out through the wire. We do not joke with the drowsy sentries who stand lines in bunkers constructed with sandbags and logs from the jungle and sheets of galvanized tin. We ignore the hundreds of grunts from the 26th Marine Regiment who are sprawled along the perimeter, ready to move out on Operation Gold. Our squad is walking point for a battalion. We ignore Claymore mines, rust-eaten Coca-Cola cans hung on the concertina wire with pebbles in them, red aluminum triangles with MINES and MIN stenciled on them, trenches full of garbage, catholes full of fly-sprinkled turds, and heaps of brass from our howitzers.

This time we do not salute Sorry Charlie. Sorry Charlie is a skull, charred black. Our gunner, Animal Mother, mounted the skull on a stake in the kill zone. We think that it's the skull of an enemy grunt who got napalmed outside our wire. Sorry Charlie is still wearing my old black felt Mousketeer ears, which are getting a little moldy. I wired the ears onto Sorry Charlie for a joke. As we hump by, I stare into the hollow eye sockets. I wait for a white spider to emerge. The dark, clean face of death smiles at us with his charred teeth, his inflexible ivory grin. Sorry Charlie always smiles at us as though he knows a funny secret. For sure, he knows more than we do.

Back on the hill, resupply choppers *wop-wop* down to earth like monster grasshoppers while mortar shells rip up the steel carpet of the airstrip.

We lock and load.

Our minds sink into our feet.

On a stump inside the treeline someone has nailed a scrap of ammo crate with crude letters that are black through the ground fog: ALL HOPE ABANDON, YE WHO ENTER HERE. We do not laugh. Our eyes stay on the trail. We have seen the sign a hundred times and believe it.

We meet some guys from India Three-Five humping down from their night ambushes. Scuttlebutt is, nobody got in the shit. No VC. No NVA. Outstanding, we all agree. Decent, we say, and we ask them if any of their sisters put out. They offer to buy us free beer if we promise to pee down our legs and we're to be sure and write if we need any help.

*Dawn.*

We come to the last two-man listening post. Cowboy waves his hand and Alice takes the point.

Alice is a black colossus, an African wild man with a sweat rag of green parachute silk tied around his head; no helmet. He wears a vest he has made from the skin of a Bengal tiger he wasted one night on

Hill 881. He wears a necklace of Voodoo bones—chicken bones from New Orleans. He calls himself "Alice" because his favorite record album is Arlo Guthrie's *Alice's Restaurant*. Cowboy calls Alice "The Midnight Buccaneer" because Alice wears a gold ring in his left ear. Animal Mother calls Alice "The Ace of Spades" because Alice sticks poker cards between the teeth of his confirmed kills. And I call Alice "Jungle Bunny" because it mocks Alice's truly savage nature.

Alice has a blue canvas shopping bag slung over his shoulder. The blue canvas shopping bag is filled with foul-smelling gook feet. Alice collects enemy soldiers; he shoots them dead, then chops their feet off.

*All clear,* says Alice with a hand signal. Alice's hands are protected by pigskin gloves. He hacks the jungle with his machete.

Cowboy waves his hand and we move along the trail, Indian-file.

Cowboy steps off the trail, jabs his gray Marine-issue glasses with his forefinger. In the gray glasses Cowboy does not look like a killer, but like a reporter for a high school newspaper, which he was, less than a year ago.

Humping in the rain forest is like climbing a stairway of shit in an enormous green room constructed by ogres for the confinement of monster plants. Birth and death are endless processes here, with new life feeding on the decaying remains of the old. The black earth is cool and damp and the oversized greenery is beaded with moisture, yet the air is thick and hot because the triple canopy holds in the humidity. The canopy of interwoven branches is so thick that sunlight filters through only in pale, infrequent shafts like those in Sunday-school pictures of Jesus talking to God.

Beneath mountains like the black teeth of dragons we hump. We hump up a woodcutter's trail, up slopes of peanut butter, over moss-blemished boulders, into God's green furnace, into the hostile terrain of Indian country.

Thorny underbrush claws our sweaty jungle utilities and our bandoliers and our sixty-pound field packs and our twelve-pound Durolon flak jackets and our three-pound camouflaged helmets and our six-and-a-half-pound fiberglass and steel automatic rifles. Limp sabers of elephant grass slice into hands and cheeks. Creepers trip us and tear at our ankles. Pack straps rub blisters on our shoulders and salty water wiggles in dirty worm trails down our necks and faces. Insects eat our skin, leeches drink our blood, snakes try to bite us, and even the monkeys throw rocks.

We hump, werewolves in the jungle, sweating 3.2 beer, ready, willing, and able to grab wily Uncle Ho by his inscrutable balls and never let go. But our real enemy is the jungle. God made this jungle for Marines. God has a hard-on for Marines because we kill everything we see. No slack. He plays his games; we play ours. To show our appreciation for so much omnipotent attention we keep Heaven packed with fresh souls.

Hours pass. Many, many of them. We don't know what time it is anymore. In the jungle there is no time. Black is green; green is black—we don't even know if it's night or day.

Cowboy strides up and down our line of march. He reminds us to maintain ten yards between each man. Frequently he stops to check his compass and acetate map.

We hurt. We ignore the pain. We wait for the pain to become monotonous; it does.

Our New Guy sweats and stumbles and looks like he could get lost looking for a place to shit. A heat casualty for sure. The New Guy eats pink salt tablets like a kid eating jelly beans, then gulps hot Kool-Aid from his canteen.

Monotony. Everything samey-same—trees, vines like dead snakes, leafy plants. The sameness leaves us unmoored.

The fuck-you lizards greet us: "Fuck you . . . fuck you . . ."

A cockatoo laughs, invisible, laughs as though he knows a funny secret.

We hump up rocky ravines and I can hear Gunny Sergeant Gerheim bellowing at Private Leonard Pratt on Parris Island: *The only way to reach any objective is by taking one step at a time.* That's all. Just one step. One more. One more. One more.

One more.

We think about things we will do after we rotate back to the World, about silly high-school capers we pulled before we were sucked up into the Crotch, about hunger and thirst, about R & R in Hong Kong and Australia, about how we are all becoming Coca-Cola junkies, about picking popcorn kernels out of our teeth at the drive-in movie with ol' Mary Jane Rottencrotch, about the excuses we'll have to invent for not writing home, and especially and particularly about the number of days left on each of our short-timer's calendars.

We think about things that aren't important so that we won't think about fear—about the fear of pain, of being maimed, of that half-expected thud of an antipersonnel mine or the punch of a sniper's bullet, or about loneliness, which is, in the long run, more dangerous, and, in some ways, hurts more. We lock our minds onto yesterday, where the pain and loneliness have been censored, and on tomorrow, from which pain and loneliness have been conveniently deleted, and most of all, we lock our minds into our feet, which have developed a life and a mind of their own.

*Hold*. Alice raises his right hand.

The squad stops, now, within rifle shot of the DMZ. Cowboy flexes the fingers of his right hand as though cupping a breast. *Booby trap?*

Alice shrugs. *Just cool it, man.*

Our survival hangs on our sniper bait's reflexes and judgment. Alice's eyes can detect green catgut trip wires, bouncing betty prongs, tiny plungers, loose soil, crushed plants, footprints, fragments of packaging debris, and even the fabled punji pits. Alice's ears can lock onto unnatural silences, the faint rattle of equipment, the thump of a mortar shell leaving the tube, or the snap of a rifle bolt going home. Experience and animal instincts warn Alice when a small, badly concealed booby trap has been set on the trail for easy detection so that we will be diverted off the trail into a more terrible one. Alice knows that most of the casualties we take are from booby traps and that in Viet Nam almost every booby trap is designed so that the victim is his own executioner. He knows what the enemy likes to do, where he likes to set ambushes, where snipers hide. Alice knows the warning signals that the enemy leaves for his friends—the strips of black cloth, the triangles of bamboo, the arrangements of stones.

Alice really understands the shrewd race of men who fight for survival in this garden of darkness—hard soldiers, strange, diminutive phantoms with iron insides, brass balls, incredible courage, and no scruples at all. They look small, but they fight tall, and their bullets are the same size as ours.

A lot of Marines who choose to walk point have death wishes—that's the scuttlebutt. Some guys want to be heroes and if you walk point and are still alive at the end of the patrol then you are a hero. Some guys who walk point hate themselves so much that they don't care what they do and don't care what is done to them. But Alice walks point because Alice thrives on being out front. *Sure I'm scared,* he told me one night after we'd smoked about a ton of dope, *but I try not to show it.* What Alice needs are those moments when he can see into what he calls the "beyond."

Alice freezes. His right hand closes into a fist: *Danger.*

All of Alice's senses open up. He waits. Invisible birds scatter from tree to tree. Alice grins, sheathes his machete, lifts his M-79 grenade launcher to his shoulder. The "blooper" is like a toy shotgun, comically small.

Ancient trees stand silent, a jade cathedral of mahogany columns two hundred feet high, roots entwined, branches interwoven, with thick, scaly vines roped around solid trunks.

Adrenaline gives us a high.

Alice shrugs, lowers his weapon, gives us his usual thumbs-up, *all clear;* as if to say, *I'm so cool that even my errors are correct.*

153

Cowboy's right hand slices the air again, and we all shift our gear to less painful positions and move out, grumbling, bitching. Our thoughts drift back into erect-nipple wet dreams about Mary Jane Rottencrotch and the Great Homecoming Fuck Fantasy, back into blinking black and white home movies of events that did not happen quite the way we choose to remember them, back into bright watercolor visions of that glorious rotation date circled in red on all of our short-timer's calendars—different dates—but with the same significance: *Home*.

Alice hesitates. His gloved hand reaches out and plucks an oversized yellow orchid from a swirl of vines. Standing to attention, Alice inserts the thick, juicy stem into a leather loop on his ammo vest, the skin of a Bengal tiger. In rows of loops across the front of the vest hang two dozen M-79 grenade rounds.

Alice's blue canvas shopping bag is slung over his shoulder. The bag is tattooed with graffiti, autographs, obscene doodles, and a scoreboard of stick men recording Alice's seventeen confirmed kills. On the blue canvas shopping bag are fading black block letters: *Lusthogs Delta 1/5 We Deal in Death and Yea, though I walk through the valley of death, I shall fear no evil, for I am the evil* and, in crisp new letters: DON'T SHOOT—I'M SHORT and a helmet on a pair of boots.

As he humps down the narrow trail, Alice hums, *You can get anything you want . . . at Alice's Restaurant. . . .*

Cowboy stops, turns around, sweeps a muddy pearl-gray Stetson off his head.

"Break," he says.

Green Marines in the green machine, we sit beside the trail.

"I got to souvenir me an NVA belt buckle," says Donlon, our radioman. "The silver kind with a star. Go home with something decent or the civilians will think I was a poge, punching a typewriter. I mean, I'm short—thirty-nine days and a wake-up."

I say, "That's not short. Twenty-two days and a wake-up. Count them."

"That ain't short," says Animal Mother. "Alice is short."

Alice brags: "Twelve days and a wake-up left in country, ladies. Count 'em. I *am* a short-timer, no doubt about it. Why, I'm so short that every time I put on my socks I blindfold myself."

I grunt, "Tht's not short enough, Jungle Bunny. The Doc is beaucoup short. Nine days and a wake-up. Right, Doc? You a single-digit midget?"

Doc Jay is chewing a mouthful of canned peaches. "I got to extend again."

Nobody says anything. Doc Jay won't be allowed to extend again. Doc Jay has been in Viet Nam for two years, treating major wounds with minor medical training. Doc Jay wants to save all of the wounded, even those killed in action and buried months ago. Every night dead Marines beg him to come into their graves. A week ago, our company commander picked up a football that was lying on the trail. The football blew him in half. Doc Jay tried to tie the captain back together with compress bandages. It didn't work. Doc Jay started giggling like a kid watching cartoons.

"I'm going to extend, too!" says the New Guy as he shoves his Italian sunglasses up onto his forehead. "Do you guys—?"

"Oh, screw yourself, New Guy," says Animal Mother, not looking up. Mother is holding his M-60 machine gun in his lap and is massaging the black vanadium steel with a white cloth. "You ain't been in country a week and already you're saltier than shit. You ain't been born yet, New Guy. Wait until you got a little T.I., candy ass, and then I may allow you to speak. Yeah, a little fucking time in."

"Gung ho!" I say, grinning.

Animal Mother says, "Fuck you, Joker." He starts breaking down the machine gun.

I blow Mother a kiss. Animal Mother is a swine, no doubt about it, but he's also big and mean; he inspires a certain tolerance.

"Joker thinks he has an outstanding program," Mother tells the New Guy. "Going to Hollywood after he rotates back to the World. If I don't waste him first. Going to be Paul fucking Newman. My ass." Animal Mother pulls out a deck of poker cards. The cards are dog-eared and greasy and have photographs of Tijuana whores on them. The Tijuana whores are establishing meaningful relationships with donkeys and big dogs.

Animal Mother deals draw poker hands to himself and to the New Guy.

The New Guy hesitates, then scrapes up his cards.

Animal Mother unbuckles his field pack and pulls out a brown plastic rack of poker chips—red, white, and blue. Mother takes a stack of plastic chips from the rack and drops them on the deck in front of the New Guy. "Where you from, you little shit?"

"Texas, sir."

"Sir, my ass. This ain't P.I. and there ain't no way I'm gonna be no fucking officer. Never happen. Ain't

"Yes, sir," says the New Guy, dropping two chips into the pot.

"I'm horny," I say. "I can't even get a piece of hand."

Animal Mother groans. "That was real funny, Joker. I don't get it." He drops two chips, then three more. "I raise you three bucks. Dealer takes two cards."

The New Guy says, "I'll take three cards. And I'm not a hero. Just want to do my job. You know, defend freedom—"

"Fuck freedom," says Animal Mother. Animal Mother starts reassembling the M-60. He kisses each piece before snapping it back into place. "Flush out your headgear, New Guy. You think we waste gooks for *freedom*? Don't kid yourself; this is a slaughter. You've got to open your eyes, New Guy—you owe it to yourself. If I'm gonna get *my* balls shot off for a word I get to pick my own word and my word is *poontang*. Yeah, you better believe we zap zipperheads. They waste our bros and we cut them a big piece of payback. And payback is a motherfucker."

"Why talk about it?" asks Donlon. "The Nam can kill me, but it can't make me care. I just want to get back to the land of the Big PX in one piece. I owe it to myself."

"Why go back?" I ask. "Here or there, samey-same. Home is where my sergeant is—right, Cowboy?" I turn and look at Animal Mother. "You watch Cowboy, New Guy. Cowboy will tell you what to do."

"Yeah," says Donlon, plucking a pack of cigarettes from the elastic band around his helmet. "Cowboy takes this shit seriously."

Cowboy grunts. "Just doing my job, bro, just counting my days." He smiles. "You know what I did back in the World? After school, I shucked pennies out of parking meters. I had a red wagon to pour the pennies in, and I had a blue cap with a silver badge on it. I thought I was hot shit. Now all I want is a ranch with some horses. . . ."

Animal Mother says, "Well, some cunts smell really bad, and Viet Nam smells really bad, so I say, fuck it. And fuck the lifers who invented it."

"I hear you talking," I say. "I see your lips move. But we all brown-nose the lifers. . . ."

"That's an amen," says Alice, up the trail. He swats a mosquito away from his face. "We talk the talk, but we don't walk the walk."

Donlon glares at me. "So who the hell are you? Mahatma Gandhi?" Donlon aims an index finger at me. "You're honcho of the first fire team, Joker. That makes you the assistant squad leader. So you're no different. You just like to feel superior."

"Shit."

"I wouldn't shit you, Joker. You're my favorite turd."

"*Fuck . . . you. . . .*"

"Quiet, Joker," says Cowboy. "Somebody's mother might be hiding in the bush and you're talking dirty. Keep it in the family, okay?"

"Yes. That's affirmative, Cowboy." I look at Donlon. "When Cowboy gives me the order I'll eat the boogers out of a dead man's nose. I ain't got the guts to rot in Portsmouth. I admit it. But I don't *give* orders. I—"

"Bullshit," says Donlon. "You and your fucking peace symbol. Why do you wear that thing? You're here, same as us. You're no better than we are."

"*Look,*" I say, trying not to lose my temper, "Maybe the Crotch can fuck me, but I won't spread my own cheeks."

Animal Mother interrupts: "You ain't got a hair on your ass."

My lips are trembling. "Okay, Mother, you can just eat the peanuts out of my shit. I'm not the author of this farce, I'm just acting out my role. It's bad luck to wear green on stage but the war must go on. If God had wanted me to be a Marine I'd have been born with green, baggy skin. You *got* that?"

Nobody says anything.

I say, "I'm just a snuffy. A corporal. I don't send anybody out to get blown away. I know that getting killed over here is a waste of time."

I stand up. I take three steps toward Animal Mother. "You be gung ho, Mother. You give the orders." I take another step. "But *not me!*"

Nobody says anything.

Finally the New Guy says softly, "Bet a buck."

Animal Mother looks at me, then starts dropping his chips into the pot one at a time. "Call . . . raise you. . . ." Counting . . . counting. "Five bucks."

The New Guy thinks about it. "I call."

"Oh, Jesus H. Christ!" Animal Mother slaps his cards down hard, bending them. "Number ten! I ain't got shit."

The New Guy says, "Three jacks." He flashes his cards and rakes up the pot.

"Hey, Mother," says Donlon, laughing, "that was humble."

Alice says, "You sure bluffed out the New Guy."

I say, "Lose a few, lose a few—right, Mother?"

Mother tries to be cool about it. "I couldn't fold, could I? Had over four bucks in the pot. I thought the New Guy would fold. Most people are afraid of me. . . ."

Donlon laughs again. "Your program is squared away, New Guy. What's your name?"

"Parker," says the New Guy, smiling. "Name's Parker. Henry. People call me Hank."

The New Guy counts his chips. "Animal Mother, you owe me nine and a half bucks."

Animal Mother grunts.

I say, still standing, "Lose a few, lose a few—right, Mother?"

"Who fucking asked you, Joker? You're funny enough to be a lifer."

"Yeh? Well, when I'm a civilian first class and you're a bonehead funny gunny I'll buy you a beer and then I'll kick your ass." I sit down.

Cowboy grins. "You can buy me a beer, too, Joker. But you'll have to wait until I'm twenty-one."

Down the trail, someone laughs very loud. I say, "Hey, belay that noise. I'm making all the noise for this squad."

Lance Corporal Stutten, honcho of the third fire team, gives me the finger. Then he turns to the guy who laughed—a skinny redneck named Harris—and says, "Shut the fuck up, Harris."

Animal Mother says, "Yeah, Harris, obey General Joker."

I say, "I'm ready to jump on your program, you fucking ape. . . ."

"So eat this monkey turd and choke on it, poge." Animal Mother spits. "You just can't hack—"

And then I'm on my feet, my K-bar in my hand. There's hot saliva on my lips and as I hold the big jungle knife inches from Animal Mother's face I'm snarling like an animal. "Okay, you son-of-a-bitch, I'm gonna cut your fucking eyes out. . . ."

Animal Mother looks at me, then at the blade of my K-bar, then at Cowboy. His hand moves to his M-60.

Cowboy continues to eat. "Stow that pig-sticker, Joker. You know how I feel about that Mickey Mouse shit. Now get your head and your ass wired together or—"

"No way, Cowboy. Never happen. He's been on my—"

Cowboy jabs at his glasses. "Didn't ask to run a rifle squad in this piss tube war . . . but I *will* break your back, if that's the way you play. . . ."

Donlon whistles. "Cowboy's—"

Cowboy says, "Shut up, Donlon."

I relax a little bit and then I slip my K-bar back into its leather sheath. "Yeah, yeah, I guess all this humping has given me diarrhea of the mouth."

Cowboy shrugs. "No sweat, Joker." Cowboy stands up. "Okay, ladies, stow the pogey bait. Let's saddle up. Moving."

"Moving" is repeated down the trail.

I struggle into my gear. "Hey, Animal Mother, I wasn't really going to waste you. It's just that I'm well, you know, a trained killer. Cut me a huss with my pack. . . ."

Animal Mother shrugs and helps me into my NVA rucksack. Then I help him put on his field pack. I say, "Now you buy me Saigon tea?" Mother sneers. I blow him a kiss. "No sweat, *maleen*, I love you too much." Mother spits.

Cowboy waves his hand and Alice takes the point.

I say, "Break a leg, Jungle Bunny."

Alice gives me the finger. Then he raises his right fist and throws power. On the blue canvas shopping bag slung on Alice's back is the warning: *If you can read this your too dam close.*

Cowboy waves his hand and the squad moves out. My gear feels like a bag of rocks, heavier than before.

Animal Mother tells Parker, the New Guy, "Don't follow me too close, New Guy. If you step on a mine I don't want to get fucked up."

Parker steps back.

As is my custom, I salute Animal Mother so that any snipers in the area will assume that he is an officer and shoot him instead of me. I have become a little paranoid since I painted a red bull's-eye on the top of my helmet.

Animal Mother returns my salute, then spits, then grins. "You sure are funny, you son-of-a-bitch. You're a real comedian."

"Sorry 'bout that," I say.

Searching for something we don't want to find, we hump. And hump. And when we're so bone-sore tired that our minds sever contact with our bodies, we hump even faster, green phantoms in the twilight.

From somewhere, from everywhere, an almost inaudible *snap*.

A bird goes insane. One bird sputters overhead. And a great weight of birds shifts across the canopy.

Alice stands rigid and listens. He raises his right hand and closes it into a fist. *Danger*.

I slump forward. My body is aching with all the thousand natural shocks that flesh is heir to after every fiber of every muscle is begging you to stop but you choose to overrule such objections by a force of will stronger than muscle, bullying your body into taking one more step, one more step, just one more step. . . .

Cowboy thinks about it. Then he says, "Hit it."

Wavering forms crumple to the deck as Cowboy's order is echoed from man to man back down the trail.

I say to Cowboy, "Bro, I was hoping a sniper would ding me so I'd have an excuse to fall down. I mean, I think I'm going to hate this movie. . . ."

Cowboy is watching Alice. "Cut the shit, Joker."

Kneeling, Alice studies the few yards of trail he can see before it's swallowed by leathery, dark green jungle plants. Alice studies the treetops, too, for a long time. "It's not right, bro."

I say, "That's affirm, Cowboy. All my crabs are screaming, 'Abandon ship!' 'Abandon ship!'"

Cowboy ignores me, keeps his eyes on Alice. "We got to *move*, Midnight."

The jungle is silent except for the *squeak-squeak* of a canteen being unscrewed.

"Hurry up and wait. Hurry up and wait." Alice wipes the sweat from his eyes. "All I want to do is make it back to the hill so I can smoke about one ton of dope. I mean, are you sure this is safe? I . . . wait . . . I heard something."

Silence.

"A bird," says Cowboy. "Or a branch falling. Or—"

Alice shakes his head. "Maybe. Maybe. Or maybe a rifle bolt going home. . . ."

Cowboy's voice is stern: "You're paranoid, Midnight. No gooks here. Not for maybe another four or five klicks. We got to keep moving or we'll give the gooks time to set up an ambush in front of us. You *know* that. . . ."

Donlon crawls over to Cowboy, handset at his ear. "Hey, Lone Ranger, the old man wants a report on our position."

"Let's *move*, Midnight. I mean it."

Alice rolls his eyes. "Feets, get movin'." Alice takes one step forward, then hesitates. "I can remember when I've had more fun."

I say in my John Wayne voice: "Viet Nam is giving war a bad name."

Daddy D. A., who's walking tail-end Charlie, calls out: "HEY, MR. VIET NAM WAR, WE HOME-STEADING?"

Cowboy says, "Everybody shut the fuck up."

Alice shrugs, mumbles, takes another step forward. "Cowboy, m'man, maybe old soldiers never die, but young ones do. It ain't easy being the black Errol Flynn, you know. I mean, if I don't get the Congressional Medal of Honor for all the crazy shit I do, I am going to send Mr. L. B. J. an eight-by-ten photo of my black bee-hind, with a caption on the back, telling him what it is. . . ."

Alice, the point man, moves out. He ditty-bops into a little clearing. "I mean—"

*Bang.*

The crack of an SKS sniper's carbine jolts Alice into a rigid position of attention. His mouth opens. He turns to speak to us. His eyes cry out.

Alice falls.

"HIT IT!"

Falling forward—*now.* . . .

"Oh, no. . . ." Black earth.

Dead leaves. "ALICE!"

"What . . . ?" Damp. Bleeding elbows.

"MIDNIGHT!"

Looking, not seeing, looking. . . .

"Oh-oh . . . Shit City. . . ."

Waiting. Waiting. "Hey, man. . . ."

Silence.

My guts melt.

"ALICE!"

Alice doesn't move and I curl up and try to make myself small and my asshole feels like it has been turned inside out and I think how wonderful it would be if Chaplain Charlie had taught me magic and then I could crawl up into my own asshole and just disappear and I think: *I'm glad it's him and not me.*

"ALICE!"

Alice, the point man, is down. His big black hands are locked around his right thigh. On the deck all around him are a dozen decayed gook feet.

Blood.

"FACE OUTBOARD!"

Cowboy says, "Damn." He shoves his Stetson to the back of his head and jabs at his glasses with his index finger. "CORPSMAN UP!"

Cowboy's command is echoed back down the trail.

Doc Jay comes scrambling up on all fours like a bear in a hurry.

Cowboy waves his hand. "Come on, Doc."

Donlon grabs Cowboy's ankle, tries to hand Cowboy the radio handset. "Colonel Travis is on the horn."

"Fuck off, Tom. I'm busy."

Cowboy and Doc Jay start crawling.

Donlon says into the handset: "Uh, Sudden Death Six, Sudden Death Six, this is Baby Bayonet. Do you copy? Over."

Cowboy stops crawling, calls back: "Gunships. And a med-evac."

Donlon talks into the handset, talks to the old man. *Static.* The handset hangs on a wire hook attached to Donlon's helmet strap. Donlon's singsong words are like a prayer he has known for a long time. Donlon stops talking, listens to an insect inside the handset, then shouts: "The old man says, "Only *you* can prevent forest fires.'"

Cowboy looks back. "What? What the hell does *that* mean?"

The radio crackles. *Static.* "Uh . . . say again, say again. Over." *Static.* Donlon listens, nodding. Then: "I roger that. Stand by, one." Donlon yells: "The old man keeps saying, 'Only *you* can prevent forest fires.' . . ."

Cowboy crawls back to our position. "Donlon, boy, if you're fucking with me. . . ."

Donlon shrugs. "Scouts honor."

I say, "Cowboy, are you absolutely sure that the colonel is on our side?"

Animal Mother spits. "There it is. He's a lifer, ain't he?"

Donlon shakes his head. "No slack. The old man is *dinky-dow*, crazy."

I grunt. "Sanity is overrated."

Cowboy says, "Just tell that lifer son-of-a-bitch that I need a dustoff for—"

*Bang.*

A rifle bullet snaps through Donlon's radio. The impact of the bullet flips Donlon onto his back. Donlon struggles like an overturned turtle.

I crawl on my hands and knees. I grab Donlon's rifle belt. I drag him behind a boulder.

Donlon swallows air. "Beaucoup thanks, bro. . . ."

Cowboy and Doc Jay are arguing. Cowboy says, "Alice is in the open. We can't reach him."

The New Guy says, "Is it just one enemy soldier?"

"Shut your mouth." Animal Mother sets up his M-60 machine gun on a rotten log and adjusts a golden ammo belt over a C's can he has attached to the gun so that the rounds feed in smoothly.

Cowboy says, "I got to send back a runner—"

*Bang.*

Cowboy rolls over. "I'm okay. I'm okay."

"He hit Alice again!"

Alice moves, groans. "It hurts . . . it hurts. . . ."

There's a dark hole through the canvas jungle boot on Alice's left foot. Alice laughs, grins, grits his teeth. "I'm short. . . ."

Animal Mother kicks the rotten log and opens fire. High-velocity machine-gun bullets clip, chop, and ricochet through the canopy, snapping into tree trunks with rhythmic precision, cutting leaves from twigs and killing birds.

The New Guy opens up with his M-16. Lance Corporal Stutten fires an M-79 and the grenade bursts, invisible in the darkness. I see a strange shadow on a limb so I throw a few rounds in there with my grease gun. But it's Maggie's drawers. There's nothing to shoot at.

The New Guy pops a frag and lobs it in.

Cowboy screams into the jarring thud: "OKAY, OKAY, EVERYBODY FUCKING COOL IT."

Everyone stops firing—everyone except Animal Mother. I put my hand on Mother's shoulder but his weapon continues to spill hot brass and black metal links until the belt runs out.

"We gotta *kill* that cocksucker!" says Animal Mother. "Payback is a motherfucker!"

"Yeah."

"Yeah."

"The law of the jungle, man."

Animal Mother punches the rotten log with his fist. "I'll punch his fucking heart out!"

"Yeah."

"Kill that cocksucker!"

Alice is trying to crawl to cover. "Cowboy? Bro?" Alice extends his gloved right hand.

*Bang.*

Alice's hand is knocked down. He lifts it again slowly. Ragged leather. And Alice's right forefinger is missing. "Oh, no . . . not . . ."

Alice screams.

Doc Jay stands up. Cowboy grabs him and pulls him down. "You crazy?" But Doc Jay wrestles free. He unhooks the Unit One medical kit from his web belt and drops the rest of his gear.

Cowboy looks sick. "Don't try it, bro. That sniper does not miss. . . ."

"*I'm* the corpsman," says Doc Jay. "Not you." And before Cowboy can react, Doc Jay is on his feet and running. He runs at a crouch, zigzagging.

*Bang.*

Doc Jay stumbles, falls.

The Doc's left thigh has been torn open. Jagged bone protrudes. The Doc tries to push himself forward with his good leg.

Cowboy pops a smoke grenade, lobs it in.

"We've got to *do* something. . . ."

The squad bunches up behind the boulder. "Spread out," I say, halfheartedly. The New Guy is watching with wild eyes, his weapon held at port arms. Animal Mother's bloodshot eyes scan the canopy for muzzle

170

flashes, movement, any sign of life. Lance Corporal Stutten and the rest of the squad watch silently—they are waiting for orders. Donlon is hugging his dead radio.

Doc Jay stands up, balances himself on his good leg. He bends over and hooks Alice under the armpit with his forearm, tries to lift him.

*Bang.*

Doc Jay collapses. Now his left foot is a bloody lump. He waits for the last bullet. When the last bullet doesn't come he sits up, pulls Alice across his lap. The Doc fumbles in his Unit One, takes out a Syrette, gives Alice a hit of morphine.

Using his teeth, Doc Jay tears the waxy brown wrappers off three compress bandages. The Doc ties the bandages around Alice's wound. Alice groans, says something we can't hear. Doc Jay uses his shirttail to wipe the sweat from Alice's forehead, then pulls out a piece of rubber tubing he uses to tie tourniquets.

*Bang.*

Doc Jay's right hand is shattered. The Doc tries to move his fingers.

He can't.

Green smoke pours from Cowboy's smoke grenade, obscuring the clearing.

Cowboy starts to tell us what to do. But he can't make up his mind. Then: "We're pulling out. That's a shitty thing to do, but we can't refuse to accept the situation. We saw this in Hue. That sniper is just sucking us in. Wants the whole squad, one at a time. You *know* that. Doc and Midnight are wasted; we're not. Saddle up."

Nobody moves.

Cowboy stands up. "Do it."

We all know that Cowboy is right. He's hard, but he's right.

"GET SOME!"

Without warning, the New Guy charges for the clearing. He fires blind. He lopes along with the fluid grace of a meat eater, a predator attacking. His chin is dripping saliva. The New Guy wants warm blood to drink. The New Guy wants human flesh to tear apart and devour. The New Guy's eyes are red; the New Guy's eyes glow in the shadow world around us. He fires blind. The New Guy doesn't know what the hell he's doing. He thinks he's John Wayne. He hasn't been born yet.

Cowboy tries to trip the New Guy as he double-times up the trail, but the New Guy catches his balance and runs faster, a werewolf charging into the house of death. He stumbles up to Doc Jay. He spins around. His red eyes probe the canopy. "Com'on, Doc. I'll help you. I'll carry—"

*Bang.*

For a breath or two we think maybe the sniper has missed for the first time. Then the New Guy drops to his knees, praying, clutching his throat.

Cowboy says, "Let's *move.*"

"Move, my ass," says Animal Mother. "*You* move, motherfucker."

Cowboy takes a step toward Animal Mother, puts his face up close to Animal Mother's face, looks Animal Mother right in the eye. "Mother, take the point."

Animal Mother stands up, pulls his machine gun off the log and sets the butt into his hip so that the black barrel slants up at a forty-five-degree angle.

"Marines *never* abandon their dead or wounded, Mr. Squad Leader, *sir*."

Cowboy glares at Animal Mother for several deep breaths, then pulls me aside. "Joker, you're in charge. Move these people out," Cowboy sees that Animal Mother is listening so he adds, "Order Mother to walk the point."

Animal Mother spits.

Cowboy says in a low voice: "Never turn your back on Mother. Never cut him any slack. He fragged Mr. Shortround."

I say, "What about you, Cowboy? I mean, if you get yourself wasted who will introduce me to your sister?"

Cowboy looks at me. His face is without expression. "I don't have a sister. I thought you knew that." Cowboy looks at Doc and Alice and the New Guy. "Mother's right. I've got to try. The sniper will see you pulling back and—"

"Hey, never happen. Fuck it. You can't *do* anything."

"Move them out, Joker. By the numbers."

"But Cowboy, I—"

"It's my *job*," Cowboy says. "It's my job. . . ." Cowboy says, as though his guts are choking him. Then: "Okay?"

I hesitate.

"Okay, bro?"

"Sure, Cowboy. I'll get them all back to the hill in one piece. I promise."

Cowboy relaxes. "Thanks, Joker." He grins. "You piece of shit."

Donlon yells: "LOOK!"

Doc Jay has the New Guy across his lap. The New Guy's face is purple. Doc Jay is kissing the New Guy's purple lips in an attempt to breathe life back into the limp body. The New Guy squirms, claws for air. Doc Jay holds the New Guy down, zips out his K-bar, cuts the New Guy's throat. Air whistles in through the crude incision, blows pink bubbles in the New Guy's blood. The New Guy bucks, wheezes, coughs. Doc Jay spills his Unit One, paws through splints, compress bandages, white tape. Then, frantic, he empties his pockets. The Doc throws everything away until he finds a ball-point pen. He stares at the ball-point pen, draws his hand back to throw the pen away, stops, looks again, unscrews the pen, inserts the biggest piece into the hole in the New Guy's throat. The New Guy sucks in air, breathes irregularly through the small plastic tube. Doc Jay puts the New Guy down on the deck, gently.

*Bang.*

Doc Jay's right ear is split. Cautiously, the Doc touches the side of his head, feels wet, jagged meat.

*Bang.*

A bullet cuts off Doc Jay's nose.

*Bang.*

A bullet passes through Doc Jay's cheeks. He coughs, spits up uprooted teeth and pieces of his gums.

Animal Mother snarls, fires his machine gun into the canopy.

"Get them back," Cowboy says. He drops his Stetson and Mr. Shortround's shotgun. He pops another smoke grenade, lobs it in. He jerks Mr. Shortround's pistol from his shoulder holster. And before I can tell Cowboy that a pistol is useless in the jungle he punches me on the shoulder like a kid and runs, feinting as wildly as the narrow trail allows.

We wait.

I know that I should be getting the squad on its feet, but I too am hypnotized.

From nowhere and from everywhere comes the sound of something laughing. We all rubberneck to see who among us is so stone-cold hard that he is enjoying a world of shit like this.

The sniper is laughing at us.

We try to pinpoint the sniper's position. But the source of the laughter is all around us. The laughter seems to radiate from the jungle floor, from the jade trees, from the monster plants, from within our own bodies.

As the dark laughter draws the blood from my veins I see something. My eyes try to focus on a shadow. Sweat stings my eyes, blurs my vision. And I see Sorry Charlie, a black skull, perched on a branch, and then I understand that only a sniper that does not fear death would reveal his position by laughing. . . .

I squint. I strain my eyes. The laughing skull fades into a shadow.

Today I am a sergeant of Marines.

I laugh and laugh. The squad freezes with fear because the sniper is laughing with me. The sniper and I are laughing together and we know that sooner or later the squad will be laughing, too.

Sooner or later the squad will surrender to the black design of the jungle. We live by the law of the jungle, which is that more Marines go in than come out. There it is. Nobody asks us why we're smiling because nobody wants to know. The ugly that civilians choose to see in war focuses on spilled guts. To see human beings clearly, that is ugly. To carry death in your smile, that is ugly. War is ugly because the truth can be ugly and war is very sincere. Ugly is the face of Victor Charlie, the shapeless black face of death touching each of your brothers with the clean stroke of justice.

Those of us who survive to be short-timers will fly the Freedom Bird back to hometown America. But home won't be there anymore and we won't be there either. Upon each of our brains the war has lodged itself, a black crab feeding.

The jungle is quiet now. The sniper has stopped laughing.

The squad is silent, waiting for orders. Soon they will understand. Soon they won't be afraid. The dark side will surface and they'll be like me; they'll be Marines.

Once a Marine, always a Marine.

Cowboy stumbles into the clearing.

"We're moving," I say, more to Mother than anyone.

Mother ignores me, watches Cowboy.

*Bang.* Right leg.

*Bang.* Left leg. Cowboy falls.

*Bang.* The bullet rips open Cowboy's trousers at the crotch. "No. . . ." Cowboy feels for his balls. He shits on himself.

Animal Mother takes a step.

Before I can make a move to stop Animal Mother a pistol pops in the clearing.

*Bang.*

Then: *Bang.*

Donlon: "HE KILLED DOC AND THE NEW GUY!"

Cowboy shakes himself to stay conscious. Then he shoots Alice through the back of the head.

*Bang.* Alice's face is blown off by the forty-five caliber bullet. Alice flops as though electrocuted.

Cowboy raises the pistol and presses the huge barrel to his right temple.

*Bang.*

The pistol falls.

The sniper has put a bullet through the center of Cowboy's right hand.

The squad bunches up behind the boulder again. I study the dirty faces of all my bearded children: Animal Mother, Donlon, Lance Corporal Stutten, Berny, Harris, Rick Berg, Hand-Job, Thunder, The Kid from Brooklyn, Hardy, Liccardi, and Daddy D.A.

"Stutten, take your people back."

Lance Corporal Stutten looks at Animal Mother, takes a step toward him. The squad is going to follow Mother and commit suicide for a tradition.

Mother checks his M-60. His face is wet with tears, Viking-wild, red with rage. "We'll go for Cowboy, give the sniper too many targets. We can save him."

I take a step into Animal Mother's path.

Animal Mother raises his weapon. He holds the M-60 waist-high. His eyes are red. He growls deep in his throat. "This ain't no Hollywood movie, Joker. Stand down or I will cut you in half. . . ."

I look into Animal Mother's eyes. I look into the eyes of a killer. He means it. I know that he means it. I turn my back on him.

Animal Mother is going to waste me. The barrel of the M-60 probes my back.

The squad is silent, waiting for orders.

177

I raise my grease gun and I aim it at Cowboy's face. Cowboy looks pitiful and he's terrified. Cowboy is paralyzed by the shock that is setting in and by the helplessness. I hardly know him. I remember the first time I saw Cowboy, on Parris Island, laughing, beating his Stetson on his thigh.

I look at him. He looks at the grease gun. He calls out: "I NEVER LIKED YOU, JOKER. I NEVER THOUGHT YOU WERE FUNNY—"

*Bang.* I sight down the short metal tube and I watch my bullet enter Cowboy's left eye. My bullet passes through his eye socket, punches through fluid-filled sinus cavities, through membranes, nerves, arteries, muscle tissue, through the tiny blood vessels that feed three pounds of gray butter-soft high protein meat where brain cells arranged like jewels in a clock hold every thought and memory and dream of one adult male *Homo sapiens.*

My bullet exits through the occipital bone, knocks out hairy, brain-wet clods of jagged meat, then buries itself in the roots of a tree.

Silence. Animal Mother lowers his M-60.

Animal Mother, Donlon, Lance Corporal Stutten, Harris, and the other guys in the squad do not speak. Everyone relaxes, glad to be alive. Everyone hates my guts, but they know I'm right. I am their sergeant; they are my men. Cowboy was killed by sniper fire, they'll say, but they'll never see me again; I'll be invisible.

"Saddle up," I say, and the squad responds. Packs are hefted up. The flap and rattle of equipment. A grunt, a growl, and the Lusthog Squad is ready to move.

I study their faces. Then I say, "Man-oh-man, Cowboy looks like a bag of leftovers from a V.F.W. barbecue. Of course, I've got nothing against dead people. Why, some of my best friends are dead!"

Silence. They all look at me. I have never felt so alive.

*Semper Fi*, Mom and Dad, *Semper Fi*, my were-wolf children. Payback is a motherfucker.

They shift their gear to more comfortable positions. They wait for an order. I pick up Cowboy's muddy Stetson.

I wave my hand and the squad moves out, moves back down the trail.

Nobody talks. We're all too tired to talk, to joke, to call each other names. The day has been too hot, the hump too long. We've shot up our share of Victor Charlie jungle plants and we are wasted.

We wrap ourselves in pastel fantasies of varied designs and "X" another day off our short-timer's calendars. We look forward to imaginary bennies: hot showers, cold beer, a fix of Coke (because things go better with Coke), juicy steaks, mail from home, and a moment of privacy in which to massage our wands, inspired by fading photographs of loving wives and girl friends back in the World.

The showers will be cold, the beer, if there is any, will be hot. No steak. No Cokes. The mail, if there is any, will not be from sweethearts. The mail from hometown America, like the half dozen letters I carry unopened in my rucksack, will say: *Write more often be careful if you think it's tough there bought this used car what a report card mother is taking shots nothing good on TV don't write depressing letters so maybe send me fifty bucks new furniture in the dining room for a ring quick buddy she's pregnant be real careful write more often* and so on and so on until you feel like you just got a Dear John letter from the whole damned world.

We hump back down the trail.

Back on the hill, Sorry Charlie, our bro, will laugh at us one more time; Sorry Charlie, at least, will greet us with a smile.

Putting our minds back into our feet, we concentrate all our energy into taking that next step, that one more step, just one more step. . . . We try very hard not to think about anything important, try very hard not to think that there's no slack and that it's a long walk home.

There it is.

I wave my hand and Mother takes the point.

# ABOUT THE AUTHOR

GUSTAV HASFORD served as a combat correspondent with the First Marine Division in Viet Nam. He now lives and works in California. This is his first novel.

# DON'T MISS
## THESE CURRENT
### Bantam Bestsellers

| | | | |
|---|---|---|---|
| ☐ | 25800 | **THE CIDER HOUSE RULES**  John Irving | $4.95 |
| ☐ | 25801 | **DARK GODS**  T. E. D. Klein | $3.95 |
| ☐ | 26554 | **HOLD THE DREAM** | $4.95 |
| | | Barbara Taylor Bradford | |
| ☐ | 26253 | **VOICE OF THE HEART** | $4.95 |
| | | Barbara Taylor Bradford | |
| ☐ | 25432 | **THE OCTOBER CIRCLE**  Robert Littel | $3.95 |
| ☐ | 23667 | **NURSE'S STORY**  Carol Gino | $3.95 |
| ☐ | 24184 | **THE WARLORD**  Malcolm Bosse | $3.95 |
| ☐ | 26322 | **THE BOURNE SUPREMACY** | $4.95 |
| | | Robert Ludlum | |
| ☐ | 26056 | **THE CLEANUP** | $3.95 |
| | | John Skipp & Craig Spector | |
| ☐ | 26140 | **WILD MIDNIGHT**  Maggie Davis | $3.95 |
| ☐ | 26134 | **THE EMBASSY HOUSE**  Nicholas Proffit | $4.50 |
| ☐ | 26142 | **MATINEE IDOL**  Ron Base | $3.95 |
| ☐ | 25625 | **A CROWD OF LOVERS**  Laddie Marshak | $3.95 |
| ☐ | 26659 | **DREAMS & SHADOWS** | $4.50 |
| | | Rosemary Simpson | |

# RELAX!
## SIT DOWN
## and Catch Up On Your Reading!

# Special Offer
# Buy a Bantam Book
# *for only 50¢.*

---

*Now you can have Bantam's catalog filled with hundreds of titles plus take advantage of our unique and exciting bonus book offer. A special offer which gives you the opportunity to purchase a Bantam book for only 50¢. Here's how!*

*By ordering any five books at the regular price per order, you can also choose any other single book listed (up to a $4.95 value) for just 50¢. Some restrictions do apply, but for further details why not send for Bantam's catalog of titles today!*

*Just send us your name and address and we will send you a catalog!*

---

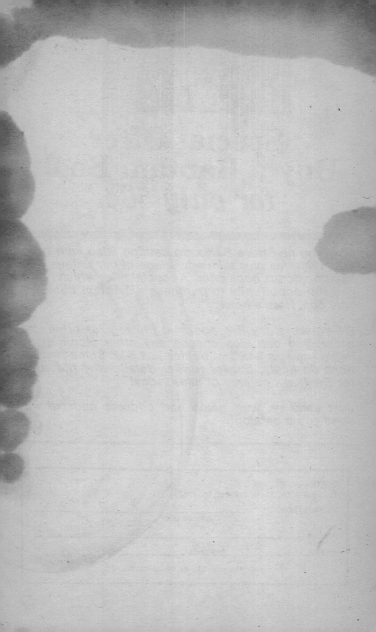